# Shaft seldom felt fear.

He felt concern. He felt apprehension. He calculated and acted with caution, planning his moves with precision and confidence that left no time or place for fear. Fear got you caught or killed when freedom and staying alive were the only objectives. John Shaft had learned long ago how to control his fears—a control that kept him out of prison and drawing breath. But driving around Harlem in a stolen police car, with a targeted gangster as his passenger, and not a shred of a plan of where to go or what to do, left Shaft feeling fear like he'd never felt before. The Grim Reaper might as well have been in the passenger seat next to him, giving him directions to Hell.

D11115571

Other John Shaft novels:

*Shaft* (1970) - Ernest Tidyman
*Shaft Among the Jews* (1971) - Ernest Tidyman
*Shaft's Big Score* (1972) - Ernest Tidyman
*Shaft Has a Ball* (1973) - Ernest Tidyman
*Goodbye, Mr. Shaft* (1973) - Ernest Tidyman
*Shaft's Carnival of Killers* (1974) - Ernest Tidyman
*The Last Shaft* (1975) - Ernest Tidyman

John Shaft graphic novels:

*Shaft: A Complicated Man* (2015) - David F. Walker

DAVID F. WALKER

# SHAFT'S REVENGE

DYNAMITE.

Edited by Hannah Elder
Cover art by Francesco Francavilla
Book design by Jason Ullmeyer


Dynamite Entertainment
113 Gaither Dr., Ste. 205
Mt. Laurel, NJ 08054
**dynamite.com**


For Dynamite:
Nick Barrucci, CEO / Publisher
Juan Collado, President / COO

Joe Rybandt, Senior Editor
Rachel Pinellas, Associate Editor

Jason Ullmeyer, Design Director
Geoff Harkins, Graphic Designer
Chris Caniano, Digital Associate
Rachel Kilbury, Digital Assistant

Rich Young, Director of Business Development
Keith Davidsen, Marketing Manager
Kevin Pearl, Sales Associate

ISBN: 978-1-60690-856-3

Publisher's Cataloging-in-Publication data
Prepared by Adrienne Bashista

Walker, David F., 1968-
    Shaft's revenge / David F. Walker.
    pages cm
    ISBN 978-1606908563

1. Shaft, John (Fictional character). 2. African American detectives --Fiction. 3. Harlem (New York, N.Y.)--Fiction. 4. Detective and mystery stories. I. Title.

PS3623.A35898 S53 2015
813.6—dc23

First printing December 2015
Printed in China

*Dedicated to Ernest Tidyman, who gave us Shaft when the world needed him the most.*

*Special thanks to Chris Clark-Tidyman, for her support in keep John Shaft alive.*

# ONE

Shaft had no idea how many women he'd been with. Sometimes, usually when he was with one of them, he'd try to figure out how many there had been. That's often what he thought about when he was with a woman—her legs open, him deep inside, his mind trying to recall all the others that had come before her.

Shaft knew that he couldn't remember all of them. He remembered faces. He remembered names. He remembered bodies, and smells, and tastes, and the way one had moaned, or how another had gasped for breath at the moment of climax, but for the most part John Shaft couldn't remember most women as an entire being. Instead, they were each like a puzzle with too many pieces missing to know what they really looked like.

Sometimes it bothered him, this fact that he had screwed so many broads, and he couldn't even recall most of them. Hell, he knew the exact number of people he'd killed. But he didn't know the number of women he'd balled.

To be sure, there were a few that he remembered. They were the ones that made an impression on him. The ones that were important enough in his life that he made room for them in his memories. There'd been the girl he lost his virginity to—Wonder Wanda. He'd been fourteen, and she'd been older, though he never knew for sure how much older. Two years? Maybe as many as five?

Shaft knew plenty of guys that had lost their virginity to Wonder Wanda. That was her specialty—her hustle—she was a cherry popper. She'd given plenty of boys in West Harlem their first taste, but as far as Shaft knew, no one got a second. And no one got it for free. Like so many others in the neighborhood, she'd figured out a way to get by. She wasn't a trick, or anything like that—at least not like some of the other ladies that sold their bodies. No, Wonder Wanda was different.

He'd never admitted it to anyone, but he'd been in love with Wonder Wanda since the moment he'd first seen her. Shaft tried to make time with other chicks, but he wanted Wanda bad enough, and to lose his virginity bad enough that he did what a lot of other guys he knew had done—stolen a bunch of food from the local grocer, and traded it for some pussy. That was her thing—Wanda traded what she had for the food she needed to feed her younger siblings. Anyone who tried to pay her in cash got turned away. And anyone who was suspected of not being a virgin didn't get any. Wonder Wanda liked them inexperienced and awkward, fumbling around her body, coming too quickly, and appreciative that she'd help them get past one of the inconveniences of adolescence.

Shaft had stolen an entire pot roast, some vegetables, and a loaf of bread. "No one's ever traded this much," Wanda told him.

Maybe that's why she gave him a second taste for free, when she never gave anyone a second taste, let alone of a third or a fourth. She told him once that she'd never been with anyone as much as she'd been with him, and that he'd been the only one to get some without offering something in return. Not that he didn't have anything to give. Shaft was too young to realize it at the time, but he'd been the closest thing to a real lover Wonder Wanda had ever had. Everyone else just fucked her.

Wonder Wanda moved away while Shaft had been locked up in juvenile detention for the first time. He never saw her again.

Shaft could still see her face in his mind as if he'd just seen her an hour earlier. And yet he couldn't remember the names or faces of so many of the others. He couldn't even remember the name of the woman lying beneath him at that moment, her legs wrapped around his waist. His mind was clouded by too much Johnny Walker Black Label, not that his poison of choice was what kept him from knowing the name of the woman whose hips thrust in unison to his.

Shaft liked to get laid, but for the most part, with a few exceptions, that's all he liked. Conversations bored him. Museums and art galleries held no interest. Going to the movies was something you did by yourself. Most important, he didn't like getting to know new people—especially women. Getting to know someone meant getting invested in them, and he couldn't do that ever again. Not after the last time.

So, he just got laid, and tried to avoid all the bullshit that came with sex, like caring and remembering. Fucking felt good. Caring and remembering led to pain. He'd endured enough pain.

He wondered what "the shrink" would say about that. She was one of the few he remembered. Dr. Monica LaSalle, a high profile psychiatrist that had been one of his clients.

Monica had hired Shaft to get the dirt on her husband, whom she suspected had been having an affair. Cases like this were no-brainers for Shaft, and he'd earned a reputation amongst Park Avenue white women whose husbands had developed a taste for something darker. These women would hire Shaft to get the proof they needed to divorce their husbands, and then some of them ended up in bed with him. Shaft figured it was their idea of revenge, inspired by their husbands dabbling on the dark side, and maybe even that movie *Behind the Green Door*.

Shaft could tell whenever he bedded a white woman that had been adventurous enough to watch the porn flick where skinny Marylyn Chambers had taken in every inch of Johnnie Keyes. All that hippie, free-love bullshit had provided a lot of white women the excuse to experiment sexually in the late 1960s, but *Behind the Green Door* had changed the game— even more so than *Deep Throat*. It made big black studs the fantasy du jour of white women who either wanted to feel something of substance between their legs, or had deep-seeded issues involving slavery.

Everywhere he went, Shaft seemed to meet some white chicks who had seen *Behind the Green Door*, and was looking to get screwed by some gangly spade with cheap-ass jungle make-up on. Shaft had no desire to don a loincloth or warrior paint on his face, but he could screw them just fine because he liked to screw.

The problem became the fact that he'd taken a few too many of these easy divorce cases, become the re-venge fuck of vindictive white women, and started to feel more like a gigolo than a private detective.

Monica LaSalle had been one of those vindictive

women. She also happened to be a psychiatrist. Most of his clients had been her clients. After several rounds of revenge against her husband, she had started talking to Shaft. At first it was pillow talk, but at some point it felt less like he was laying in bed next to a naked woman, and more like he was on some shrink's couch.

He wondered how he'd gone from getting laid to getting his head shrunk, and it didn't sit well with him. He didn't want anyone telling him that his sexual desires were really a cry for help, or whatever the fuck it was she'd said to him, between talking about abandonment issues and arrested development. Shaft sent her a bill for his services, stopped fucking her, stopped fucking the other angry Park Avenue wives, and went back to doing whatever it was he did by screwing so many women he didn't remember—including this most recent one.

Soon enough she would climax, or he would, and then they could both roll over and go to sleep. He wouldn't even have to forget her name, because he'd already forgotten.

# TWO

Knocks Persons missed Willie Joe Pierce in a way that he didn't know was possible. Willie Joe had worked for Knocks for years, making him more than a right-hand man, or top lieutenant, or chief enforcer, or whatever the hell other terms might be used to describe their relationship. For Knocks Persons, who ran the biggest crime syndicate in Harlem, Willie Joe was the son he never had—or at least the son he never claimed. There were at least a half dozen young bucks running around Harlem that may or may not have been the result of one of Persons's many conquests, but none of them stepped up to claim him as their daddy. That left Knocks in the position of being a king with no rightful heir. Willie Joe was to be that heir—the prince to an emperor that ruled Harlem like no other.

Knocks had come up with Bumpy Johnson, both working under Madame Stephanie St. Clair, and had gone to war against that Jewish motherfucker Dutch

Schultz over control of Harlem. Most people considered Bumpy to be the Godfather of Harlem, but that was bullshit. Yeah, Bumpy ruled parts of Harlem, but Knocks ruled other parts. Bumpy was a man who liked to be the center of attention, while Knocks just liked to have power. They each commanded armies and loyal subjects, and they knew how to not step on each other's toes.

Knocks had been there when Bumpy keeled over from a heart attack on July 7, 1968. On July 8th, Knocks Persons took over Bumpy Johnson's business. Blood was spilled. Enemies were made. Old niggers like Junius Tate wanted to be the boss of everything, and couldn't understand why Harlem now only needed one king, when there had been two before. More recently, there were the youngbloods—uppity niggers like Nicky Barnes and Frank Lucas, who ran around like they were in control, when in fact they all answered to the same man. They all paid taxes to Knocks Persons, even when they didn't want to.

He'd fought hard to get where he was, and though he seldom dreamed of what the future held, there had always been this notion, like a faint voice, whispering in his ear, that some day Willie Joe Pierce would take over the kingdom of Knocks Persons. That wasn't going to happen. Not with Willie Joe's head still missing, and the rest of his body scattered throughout

Harlem and the Bronx.

Someone—Knocks had no idea who—had chopped up Willie Joe like he was hog in a butcher's shop. And it wasn't just Willie Joe that had been taken out. Knocks had lost close to a dozen of his top men, and that didn't include the cats that worked under those that worked under him. Bamma Brooks had lost at least five, and it was the same for everyone in his empire. They'd all lost top men. Some had been gunned down, and in a few cases, like Willie Joe, they'd chopped up in pieces and scattered all over the city— by some mystery motherfucker with no morals. It was one thing to kill a man and dismember him, but it was another thing to not let anyone know your endgame. Unless, of course, your endgame was to have every hardcore nigger in Harlem shaking in their Stacy Adams shoes, and looking to beat a hasty retreat back down to the South, where the only thing to fear was rednecks and the Klan.

Knocks Persons wondered if Bumpy Johnson would've been scared enough to head back down to South Carolina, where he'd been born. Bumpy talked about the South like it was a special kind of Hell, one that Knocks didn't know. Persons had been born in San Juan Hill, over on the west side of Manhattan, before his grandmother moved him uptown to Harlem. Harlem was home. San Juan Hill, the worst slum in all of New York, had been torn down and replaced with the Lincoln Center. There'd be no running from Harlem, even though Knocks knew his days were numbered.

He had been stabbed, shot, and caught in an explosion. His body was covered with scars from all knocks he'd taken—knocks that had transformed him from Norville Persons, to Knocks Persons. All those scars, from all those bullets and blades, had left their mark, but none had made him afraid for his life. Life had little meaning other than the immediacy of now for Norville "Knocks" Persons—either you lived or you died. If there was a God—and Knocks wasn't even convinced he believed in God—then he was a mean motherfucker with a wicked sense of humor. Knocks had prayed when he was younger, but those prayers went unanswered, and so he had an understanding with the deity he wasn't fully convinced existed. "I won't ask you for shit, and you don't expect nothing from me," Knocks Persons said the last time he prayed.

He thought about praying for an instant. Or maybe less than an instant. But he did think about it— about asking God to watch out for him in this moment of certain doom. And then Knocks laughed at his own foolishness. Knocks knew that even if God did exist, he didn't give a shit about a nigger like him—a nigger who had his hand in so much vice and human suffering that there was a special place reserved in Hell with his own fiery throne. That is, of course, if Knocks Persons believed in Hell, which he believed in only slightly less than he believed in God.

So instead of praying for some sort of help, or some sort of salvation, or some sort of whatever-the-fuck it was people prayed for, Knocks Persons picked up the phone. God wouldn't do shit for him. But maybe, just maybe, John Shaft would help.

# THREE

Shaft lay flat on his back, staring into the darkness of his bedroom, listening to the heavy breathing of the sleeping woman lying next to him. He'd met her at the bar across the street from his apartment, the No Name, which seemed almost poetic. If he'd bothered to learn her name, he'd already forgotten it. He couldn't even remember if she was white or black.

He turned to see her naked body, illuminated by the streetlight that streamed into his room from the window that overlooked Jane Street. Her skin was dark, but not dark enough to make her black. Maybe she was mixed—some tragic mulatto that had wandered into the No Name, and ended up back at Shaft's place, rhythmically breathing in on the up-stroke, and out on the down-stroke, until one or both of them had gotten off. Shaft couldn't even remember that much.

He looked at her, thinking her dark hair was too straight for her to be mixed—unless she had run a hot comb through her hair. But normally he wouldn't have gone for that look—at least not these days. This left him to deduce that his nameless partner must've been Puerto Rican, or Costa Rican, or something along those lines. Shaft had a vague memory of her saying something about one of those tiny islands in the Atlantic, of course, he could've been confusing her with someone else.

The phone rang in the other room, distracting Shaft from the nagging thought that he didn't know the name or ethnic origin of the woman he'd just screwed. And with her sleeping on her stomach, her face half buried in one of his down feather pillows, he didn't even know what she looked like. If it weren't for the ringing phone, he'd likely get caught in the quicksand of thought that threatened to drown him every time he did this sort of thing. Fortunately, the ringing phone saved Shaft from being overwhelmed by the wave of thoughts crashing down against the rocky, jagged shore of his mind.

He got up from bed, naked, and walked to the living room. It wasn't until just before he picked up the black receiver that it occurred to him that the phone should not have been ringing. The phone seldom rang in his apartment, because so few people had his number. Some called the office, but most called the We Never Sleep So You Can Answering Service, where women he'd never met took messages and then relayed them back whenever he got around to checking in. Shaft didn't know how many people had his home number, but it wasn't many. And none of them would be calling at this hour—not that he knew the actual time. He just knew that it was still dark out, and that he'd left the No Name with the chick with no name around midnight, and screwed for at least an hour or more, before she fell asleep, and he lay awake thinking about whether or not he was fucked up in the head. That meant it was anywhere between two and four in the morning.

No one ever called him at that hour, especially not the handful of people that knew his number.

"Yeah," said Shaft into the receiver, no other greeting or salutation offered.

"I need your help," said the voice on the other end. The voice was deep, with a heavy rasp—like a rumble of thunder mixed with the sound of two bricks being rubbed together.

The voice on the other end of the phone offered no introduction, not that Shaft needed any. He knew the voice. He just had no idea how Knocks Persons had gotten his home number, or why he was calling.

"You need my help?" Shaft asked. He realized he was trying to sound like he'd just woken up, hoping that sounding tired and groggy might hide any sound of surprise that Knocks had called. It was like those people who called in sick to work, and tried to sound sicker than they were, just so no one would question their health.

"Right now," said Persons.

"Okay. I'll get dressed and hop in a cab."

"No," said Knocks. "Bamma Brooks'll be there to scoop you up in a few minutes."

With that, Knocks Persons hung up.

Shaft wondered why Bamma Brooks was coming to get him. Why not Willie Joe Pierce? In all of his dealings with Knocks Persons, Willie Joe had always been the one assigned to work with Shaft. When Persons had hired Shaft to rescue his kidnapped daughter, he'd sent Willie Joe to ride shotgun. And in his handful of other dealings with Persons, Shaft always worked with Willie Joe.

Bamma Brooks wasn't even part of the Knocks Person's inner-circle. Brooks ran his own little fiefdom within the larger kingdom of Persons. Everyone had their territories and their rackets—Brooks, Barnes, Lucas, all of them—but they were all ruled by King Knocks.

Shaft picked up the clothes that had dropped to the floor when he'd returned with the woman now asleep in his bed. They stripped down in the living room, leaving their clothes on the floor, as he carried her into the bedroom, lay her down, and slid inside of her. She'd gasped when he entered her, like so many of them gasped, as if his manhood had somehow managed to push the air out of their lungs. He liked that sound more than any other sound—even the sound some of them made during orgasm. The sounds of climax, the dirty talk, the post-copulation conversation— all of that varied from partner to partner. But the gasp was always the same.

He thought about waking her, as he got dressed, just as he thought about putting on clean, fresh clothes. Neither seemed worth the energy. She could sleep off whatever it was she'd had to drink, and wake up hung over and sore, wondering where the fuck she was, and what happened to the black stud she'd balled the night before. And Knocks Persons could put up with a man dressed in clothes that stunk of booze and cigarettes, with just a hint of coitus thrown in to make the story interesting.

Shaft smiled at the thought of walking in the office of Knocks Persons, and the gangster saying to him, "Nigger, is that pussy I smell on you?" It would make for a great anecdote in the book he would never get around to writing, made all the more funny by the fact that he couldn't even remember the name of the woman whose pussy Knocks could smell. He chuckled. Or maybe he just thought about chuckling, the same way he thought about writing the book he'd never write, or waking the woman asleep in his bed that he'd never see again.

Shaft glanced out of the living room window as he pulled a sweater over his head. Remembering how cold it had been these last few days, he wondered if he needed to wear a coat as well. Outside on Jane Street, he saw a car pull up in front of his building.

He pulled a twenty-dollar bill from his pocket, and placed it in the purse of the nameless woman sleeping in the next room. If he really wanted to, he could've checked inside for some identification—something to remind him of the name he may or may not have ever known. He also could've left some kind of note— something letting her know that the cash was for cab fare, and not payment for services rendered. For a brief moment, it bothered him that what's-her-name might've thought Shaft had placed such little value on something as precious as the sacred place she's let him explore. He left the cash for cab fare, without leaving a note. She'd be gone when he got back. Or she'd still be there. Some of them stuck around a while. It didn't matter to him either way.

Shaft grabbed the keys to the apartment and clutched them tight. He cared more about the keys than anything in the apartment itself. Grabbing his coat, he closed the door behind him, and headed down three flights of stairs, out on to the dark street where Bamma Brooks waited to take John Shaft to see Knocks Persons.

# FOUR

Shaft reached into the inside breast pocket of his coat, pulling out a half pack of cigarettes. He had a cigarette out of the pack, and inches from his lips, when he remembered that Bamma Brooks didn't allow smoking in his car. The cigarette returned to the pack, the pack to the inside coat pocket, and Shaft's mind to his last encounter with Bamma Brooks.

Shaft had a complex relationship with Brooks, just like he had a complex relationship with Persons. It was difficult to have relationships with men like that, and not have things be complex. Shaft preferred his relationships as uncomplicated as possible. That's how he kept it with women—simple and uncomplicated. He couldn't do that, however, with men like Persons or Brooks, who knew where bodies were buried.

"Since when does Knocks have you playing chauffeur?" Shaft asked. He tried to make the question sound as cordial as possible—like he really cared. Caring, and small talk, were not among Shaft's greater social skills.

Brooks cast a sideways glance at Shaft as he turned the car right, heading north on Greenwich Street, steering towards Tenth Avenue. "How 'bout I pull over, and make your black ass drive me?" asked Brooks.

"Sorry, man. Wasn't trying to start no shit. Just not used to seeing anyone other than Willie Joe doing this kind of work."

"You ain't heard?" asked Brooks.

Shaft wanted to tell Brooks that he had better things to concern himself with than the lives of Harlem gangsters. Instead, he asked, "Heard what?"

"Willie Joe is dead."

It took a lot to surprise Shaft, and even more to let the surprise show. As far as tough motherfuckers went, Willie Joe was amongst the toughest. Tough and dependable. He'd kept Shaft's ass from getting killed at least once, and as far as gangsters went, he was an okay cat. Willie Joe and Shaft would never be drinking buddies, but they'd gone to battle together, and come out the other side with minimal damage.

"What happened?" asked Shaft.

"Nigger got his ass chopped up into a dozen pieces," said Brooks. "They still ain't found his head."

"Italians?" Shaft asked.

"No. This ain't no guinea shit. Someone's been hitting every crew in Harlem, but it ain't the Italians."

Shaft wanted to ask Brooks how he could be so certain. How did Brooks know there wasn't some formal declaration of war that the Italians had simply forgotten to declare? There were still plenty of garlic-breath motherfuckers left that were pissed off over losing East Harlem to the moulinyans—maybe they'd decided to take back what had once belonged to them.

Or maybe it was someone new trying to stake a claim in Harlem. Shaft had heard crazy stories about Japanese gangsters chopping people up with samurai swords—or some shit like that. And those Chinese cats that ran shit downtown? Fuck that. Shaft had heard enough crazy shit about those Chinese fools that he knew not to fuck with them. He'd even heard that there were restaurants down in Chinatown where they were cooking up people that had pissed off the families that ran that part of town. No thanks—he had no interest in becoming some poor sucker's take-out meal of nigger-fried rice.

"Look, kid, let me tell you something," said Brooks. "I don't know what Knocks wants you for, but between you and me, this shit is getting ugly."

"Ugly? Ugly how?"

"Ugly like before you were born ugly," said Brooks, turning the wheel of the car, left on Gansevoort, which would take them to West Street. "This is like those stories Knocks and Bumpy used to sit around and tell, about when Schultz was fucking with them."

Shaft had heard all the stories about the fight to control Harlem. Every kid growing up north of 96th Street had heard the stories. Hollywood made movies about white gangsters, but the tales of black gangsters in Harlem and San Juan Hill never got turned into pictures. Instead, they were passed down through word of mouth, in barbershops and pool halls, schoolyards and speakeasies. They had become folktales—modern day myths of machine gun-toting mobsters blasting the shit out of each other all over up and down 125th Street and Lennox Avenue.

There was a sense of nostalgia—a romantic notion of how things were—that surrounded the old gangster lore of uptown. But Shaft recognized it as the undeniable fog of bullshit that clouded the reality of every ghetto in the world, and obscured the simple fact that life was cheap. And the darker the skin, the cheaper the life.

The fact of the matter was that shit had always been ugly in Harlem for folks with dark skin—and in New York—ever since the first honkies traded some shiny trinkets to some unsuspecting Indians, and then proceeded to give the poor redskin bastards small pox and syphilis for good measure. The fact that some people looked at the days of Bumpy Johnson and Knocks Persons seizing control of Harlem from some Jews and Italians with any sense of nostalgia made Shaft want to laugh as much as it made him want to vomit.

He thought about how some day people would wax rhapsodic about the days when he was younger, robbing and stealing anything he could get his hands on. There were already people who probably talked with nostalgic whimsy about gangs like the Black Knights and the 125th Street Spades, as if they were anything more than what they were, or what Shaft himself had been. They were victims of the plague of poverty and neglect, which infected poor kids with dark skin, and turned them into predators that preyed on their neighbors.

Shaft had been one of those predators. He mugged old women. Robbed stores. He'd beaten ass, had his ass beaten, and seen enough to know that there was never a time—not a single second of a single day—when ugly shit hadn't gone down in Harlem.

"It's always been ugly up 'round Harlem," said Shaft.

Brooks grunted a response that was neither agreement nor argument, but simply acknowledgment. He enjoyed conversation about as much as Shaft, and anything that resembled debate even less. His reputation as a man of few words, who let his fists do the talking, had started when he was still a boxer. When he became the chief enforcer for Junius Tate, Bamma Brooks became known as something of a silent menace. If Tate sent Brooks after your ass, the time for talking had long since passed. In those days, conversations with Brooks were one-sided exchanges that consisted of his victims begging for mercy, while his hands spoke the universal language of violence.

Brooks drove in silence, while Shaft rode in the same state. Enough history had been shared by the two men that they could've talked all the way to Harlem, across the river into the Bronx, and still have things to say by the time they reached New Rochelle. Some men liked to brag about the blood they spilled. Shaft wasn't one of those men. Neither was Brooks. And so they didn't say a word to each other as they headed north, eventually turning right on to 135th Street.

# FIVE

The first time Shaft saw the home of Knocks Persons, he couldn't believe it. Eight or nine years old, having already bounced around from more foster homes than he cared to remember, young John Shaft didn't know there were homes like that in the same world he lived in, or that colored people lived like that. He'd heard of Knocks Persons—every kid in Harlem knew the name Knocks as well as they knew the name Bumpy—but seeing the home of Persons for the first time, Shaft thought to himself that it was the home of a king.

Shaft's impression of Persons's home changed over the years, altering as his perception of the world became more grounded in the harsh reality of his surroundings. By the time he first walked through the front door of Knocks Persons's home—a door guarded by only the most trusted guns-for-hire a crime lord could keep on his payroll—Shaft no longer viewed the home or its owner as royalty, because in his mind, royalty implied some modicum of benevolence.

As Bamma Brooks neared the massive house of Knocks Persons, Shaft noticed three things. There was no guard standing at the front door, which was open, and all the lights in the grand palace were off. There were always lights on somewhere in Castle Persons, because men like Knocks knew the dangers that lurked in the shadows. Entire empires had been built in the shadows of alleys with no streetlights, and the corridors of tenement projects where the burned out light bulbs never seemed to be replaced. Men like Knocks Persons thrived in the shadows as much as they avoided them, lest they fall victim to the danger obscured by the darkness.

Brooks reached into his coat, pulling out a hand-cannon manufactured by Colt as he stopped the car. Shaft didn't bother to point out that Brooks had double-parked.

"Glove compartment," said Brooks.

Shaft leaned forward, opened the glove compartment, and pulled out a small, Saturday-night special. Far from being his weapon of choice, Shaft would make do with the .38 revolver. He had no choice. He'd given up the right to choose the moment he stepped out of his apartment building in the West Village, and rode with Brooks all the way up to Harlem.

He cursed himself, running down a long list of decisions that led to him opening the passenger-side car door, revolver in hand, crouching low so as to avoid being seen by whatever was hiding in the shadows. If only he hadn't answered the phone. If only he had remembered the name of the chick laying in his bed. Fuck, he thought to himself, I'm about to walk into a deathtrap, and I can't even remember the name of the last woman I screwed.

Shaft and Brooks made eye contact. Brooks made a motion with his hands indicating, as near as Shaft could tell, that he should follow behind the older man. Shaft was cool with Brooks taking point, because that meant the first bullets from the shadows would have a target that wasn't named John Shaft.

Both men crouched low, moving quickly toward the darkened house. A body lay splayed out on the front stoop—one of Person's guards, perforated by multiple gunshot wounds.

Shaft recognized the man as Cookie Venable. They'd come up together, running in the same gang, fighting in the same fights. A lifetime ago, Cookie was what passed for a good friend in the life of John Shaft. They hadn't seen each other since Shaft joined the Marines a decade earlier.

With at least a half dozens holes in him, all seeping the last of the blood from his body, Cookie clung to life. His breathing came in quick, shallow gasps Shaft had heard countless times in Vietnam.

Cookie looked up, his eyes, streaming with tears of pain and fear and the knowledge that his time on Earth was coming to an end, and he recognized Shaft.

"Johnny…" Cookie said, his voice a faint whisper, wet with blood, closer to death than to life.

Shaft reached out and took Cookie's hand, holding it more gently than he'd ever held the hand of a lover. Shaft had done it more times than he cared to remembered, and he knew that there probably wasn't anything more intimate than holding on to someone as they died. He'd done it with his fellow Marines, he'd done it with more than a few Vietnamese, and now, on the front stoop of Knocks Persons's house, he was doing it with one of the few people left alive that knew him when he was a kid.

"It's gonna be okay, Cookie," Shaft whispered. "Just close your eyes, and let go."

Brooks gave Shaft a hardened look that said, "We don't have time for this shit."

Shaft gave him an equally hard look that said, "Fuck you."

"R…R…Red…" gasped Cookie.

"No, man. Red ain't here," whispered Shaft. He assumed Cookie was calling out for Red Linny, who had been part of the gang they all ran with in their youth.

"Sorry, you've only got my black ass here with you now."

Cookie Venable died. His hand, like the rest of his body, went slack, slipping from the grip of the childhood friend he hadn't seen in ten years. Whatever gentleness Shaft had demonstrated with Cookie disappeared, like a light being turned off. He looked over at Brooks, and with a slight nod of his head, Shaft seemed to say, "Now."

Bamma Brooks's blood ran cold at the look in the eyes of John Shaft. Brooks had looked into the eyes of plenty of killers—cold-blooded psychopaths that placed no value on human life. The thing that terrified Brooks was that Shaft had the same cold-blooded stare, but behind that icy gaze, deeper at the core of his being, was a fire of something—compassion maybe—that actually valued human life. Killers without a cause were dangerous, but they were machines that were predictable. Men like Shaft were rare indeed—killers with a cause. Those kind of motherfuckers scared the hell out of Brooks.

Shaft followed Brooks into the dark, silent house of Knocks Persons. In a city like New York, and a neighborhood like Harlem, the silence inside the house was deafening. It meant that death was lurking in the shadows of the three-story brownstone, and that everyone and everything in the vicinity was keeping quiet, just in case the Grim Reaper decided to call on them. Shaft had no doubt that everyone within a block of the house knew what was going on—they had to—and they were cowering in fear, huddled in corners and behind furniture that offered the best protection from stray bullets. Christ, Shaft thought, this is the same thing people do in 'Nam.

Inside the foyer of the house, two more bodies lay dead. Shaft didn't recognize either man, but in the darkness, he could see the look on Brooks's face. Shaft wondered if it was the same as his own look, a few moments earlier, when he recognized Cookie Venable.

Shaft gently tapped Brooks. He pointed toward the flight of stairs leading up to the second floor, cloaked in pitch black. Brooks shook his head, and pointed down. The office of Knocks Persons was located in the basement of the house. It was also the most heavily fortified place in the building. If there was any chance Persons was still alive, he would have to be inside the refuge of his basement office.

Brooks motioned for Shaft to follow him. Both moved slowly, trying to adjust to the darkness. They both lurched with a start at the sound of gunshots coming from the basement. A second later, they heard a scream coming from upstairs, and a round of gunshots from the second floor.

Shit, fuck, and damn, Shaft thought. There are

shooters on both sides of us. We're so fucked.

A voice from the darkness seemed to confirm what Shaft was thinking.

"Looks like you motherfuckers showed up just in time to die," growled the voiced.

That's when the shooting started.

# SIX

His warrior instincts kicking into high gear, Shaft dropped to the floor, grabbing Brooks by the arm and dragging him down as well. Most shooters—especially untrained shooters—fired straight ahead. Shaft's best chances for survival were down low, on the floor, below the line of fire.

Muzzle flashes lit up the darkened foyer like flashes of deadly lightening, accompanied by the thunderous bang bang bang symphony of a full-blown firefight. Shaft counted at least four shooters, and by the amount of lead each was throwing, they had to be armed with automatics. He cursed the revolver in his hand, and its six shots. Six chances to stay alive. What the fuck was Brooks thinking? It was 1972, only old men and flat-foot cops carried revolvers these days.

Shaft and Brooks untangled themselves, each scurrying on the floor for some semblance of cover, and a better vantage point. Shaft rolled over to a coat rack standing against the wall. Brooks crawled to a small, ornate table with fresh cut flowers in a vase imported from China.

Brooks fired in the direction of one of the shooters. The flash from his muzzle betrayed his hiding place. A second later, bullets exploded the vase full of flowers. The second after that, Shaft heard a series of shots, followed by the near instantaneous swearing of Brooks, and a feeling of something hot and wet splattering on his face. Brooks had been shot.

Shaft reached out into the darkness, grabbing Brooks who lay only a few feet away, and dragged the man toward him. Bullets tore into the floor where Brooks had laid only an eighth of a second earlier. Bits of marble exploded mere inches from Brooks and Shaft.

Shaft zeroed in on where he believed two of the shooters were—one at the top of the stairs, the other in the parlor to the right of the foyer. He knew there were at least two other shooters—one down the hall and to the left, near the kitchen, and the other to the right, by the stairs leading to the basement. The shooters at the top of stairs and in the parlor were the more immediate threat. There was less cover from their line of fire, and if any bullets were to catch Shaft, they'd likely come from one of those two motherfuckers.

"You alive?" Shaft whispered.

"Yeah," said Brooks.

"Hate to tell you this," said Shaft, "but that ain't going to last long. When I move, you fire down the hall toward the kitchen."

Shaft didn't wait for Brooks to respond. Crouching in the darkness, he scurried away from Brooks, who immediately started firing his gun toward the kitchen.

The shooter at the top of the stairs fired at Brooks's position, giving Shaft a clear idea of where he stood. Shaft fired once at the shooter at the top of the stairs. The man let out a gasp as his body dropped, tumbling down the stairs. If the bullet from Shaft's gun didn't kill him, his neck snapping as he tumbled down the stairs finished him off.

Startled by their companion falling down the stairs, the remaining shooters started firing wildly. Shaft used the momentary confusion to his advantage. He leapt at the parlor shooter, firing the revolver twice. Shaft's body slammed into the parlor shooter, the two men dropped to the floor and wrestled for a moment, before Shaft fired his fourth bullet, point blank, into the man's chest.

Behind him, Shaft heard a barrage of gunfire, and Brooks swearing. Shaft wondered if the aging gangster had finally realized how stupid it was to carry a revolver, as he had no doubt run out of bullets in the middle of a gunfight.

Shaft pried the gun from the parlor shooter's hand. He didn't know how many bullets were left, but he hoped it was more than two left in his revolver.

"I got two of your friends!" Shaft shouted into the darkness. "Let's get this shit over with!"

He strained to hear the hushed whispers of the two other shooters. The words were a jumbled mess, drowned out by the pounding of Shaft's heart, and the ringing echo in his ears from all the shots fired. Shaft couldn't make out what the shooters were saying, but it sounded like they were arguing.

What kind of killers argue in the middle of a firefight, Shaft thought to himself. He crawled on his belly toward the corpse at the bottom of the stairs, and pried the gun from his hands. Shaft now had three guns, and at least two bullets. He had no time to check the automatic pistols he'd confiscated from his victims. Instead, he tucked one into the waist of his pants, and gripped the other with is left hand. Shaft could fire with his left, but he felt more comfortable with the revolver and its two bullets in his right, which offered better odds of him hitting a target.

With a gun in each hand, Shaft crawled over to Brooks. The older gangster lay motionless, though Shaft could hear his labored breathing. Brooks must've caught another slug—maybe more than one.

"Listen up, motherfuckers. I got three guns and

enough bullets to kill y'all at least three times each!" Shaft lied. Depending on his luck and his aim, he might not even have had enough bullets to kill any-one.

In the distance he could hear police sirens. There were still minutes away, and he couldn't believe it had taken them this long to respond to this much gunfire. But then again, they were in Harlem. And this was the home of Knocks Persons. For all Shaft knew, the killers in the house might've been cops, though he doubted it. Their pattern of firing was too sloppy, and the way the two were arguing from the kitchen and the stair-way leading to the basement told Shaft these cold-blooded killers were disorganized. They'd come prepared to kill, but not to fight.

"Cops'll be here in about a minute!" shouted Shaft. "Time to either go down fighting, or get hauled off like a punk!"

For the first time since he and Brooks had pulled up to the house—which couldn't have been more than four or five minutes earlier—Shaft felt a twinge of fear. In a minute, maybe less, he'd be caught in the crossfire between some desperate killers and the NYPD, who always shot first and never asked questions when it came to armed niggers in Harlem.

A loud roar, like a charging rhino, came from the end of the corridor, as one of the shooters raced down the hall toward the front door, his gun blasting straight ahead. It was the move of a desperate amateur that earned the shooter the last two bullets from Shaft's revolver.

The shooter dropped to the floor in the doorway, landing inches from the body of Cookie Venable. Shaft turned back toward the hallway, raising his arm to protect his head just as someone hit him hard. Shaft winced in pain from the blow of a cast-iron frying pan that could've crushed his skull. The force of the blow knocked the empty revolver from his right hand.

His attacker dropped the frying pan as he raced out of the house and took off down the street.

Shaft picked himself up, and took off after the last of the shooters. He transferred the gun in his left hand to his right, aimed as best as he could while running, and swore when the gun clicked empty. Tossing it to the side, he slowed down just long enough to retrieve the third gun from the waist of his pants. If he believed in praying, Shaft would've prayed that the weapon still had bullets.

# SEVEN

From his position in the basement that served as both office and underground fortress for Knocks Persons, Red Linny heard the gunfire. He heard the shouts and the screaming and the pandemonium, and none of it fazed him. Clearly, someone had shown up to save Knocks Persons, but it was too late for that shit. Knocks Persons, the undisputed Kingpin of Harlem, the last of the old school gangsters, the ugly-ass motherfucker that ran shit like it was still 1930-whenever-the-fuck, was dead.

Red Linny had expected the old man to beg for his life. Shit, everyone begged for their life when the moment came. Everyone, that is, except for Knocks Persons. Knocks didn't beg. He looked a bit surprised, though Red Linny couldn't tell where the surprise was coming from. He'd met Persons a few times, so maybe that was it. Maybe Persons was surprised that death had come calling in the form of a poot-butt nigger like Red Linny. That's what Persons had called him—to his face. The old gangster had cast a fleeting glance at Red Linny, and dismissed him, calling him a poot-butt nigger in front of everyone. If Red Linny hadn't already been planning to kill Persons then, he would've added him to the list. But Persons was already on the list.

So, maybe that was why Knocks Persons looked so surprised when Red Linny limped into the office. The limp made people laugh at him. Made them underestimate him. Made them never think of him—with his slight frame, light complexion, and fucked up limp—as anything other than a joke from around the block.

The momentary look of surprise on Persons' face made Red Linny feel good. One more 'bout-to-die-motherfucker that had underestimated him. It was the look that came after the momentary surprise that almost left Red Linny unsettled. After the look of shock flitted across the face of Knocks Persons, the old gangster smiled and let out a gentle chuckle. Persons never smiled. And he seldom laughed, let alone chuckled, and that was almost enough to throw Red Linny off his game. Almost being the operative word.

"The fuck you chucklin' at, old man?" asked Red Linny.

Knocks Persons slowly shook his massive

head, smiling like he never smiled before. "Shoulda known it would be a nigger like you," said Person. "Hi-yella faggots like you always got something to prove."

"Tough talk for a dead man," said Red Linny. "You really want to waste your last breath talkin' shit? 'Cause this hi-yella faggot is about to fill your fat ass fulla lead."

Knocks Persons stopped smiling. "Had to happen sooner or later," said Persons, shrugging. "Might as well be you." His absolute, grim resolve might have impressed someone else, but not Red Linny.

Linny pointed his gun at Persons. He'd wanted to do more than just put a bullet through the brain of the old gangster. He wanted to chop his head off and kick it around Harlem for everyone to see and know and understand that he was, in fact, the motherfuckin' man that killed Knocks Persons. But having everyone know he killed Knocks wasn't as important as getting it over with, and time was of the essence. It had cost him a lot of money to buy ten minutes from the po-lice—ten guaranteed minutes that they would wait to respond once the first calls came in.

Getting past the guard at the front door had been easy. That dumb motherfucker Cookie Venable hadn't suspected a thing, and getting past him meant getting into the house. Inside the house was where the real problems would be—lots of bodies that needed to be deprived of living. There were the other guards, the mistress, and whoever else might be unlucky enough to get caught in the middle of the business. And then there was Knocks Persons himself—the man of the hour.

"Got any last words?" Red Linny asked. He always loved when someone said that in the movies. He liked asking the question, because he loved hearing people beg for their lives. It made him feel like God.

Persons eyed his would-be killer with a look that Red Linny couldn't read. "Uneasy lies the head that wears the crown," Knocks Persons said.

Disappointed that Persons would choose Shakespeare over pleading for his life, Red Linny felt robbed of the moment. He'd honestly expected Persons to beg. "Really? That's all you've got to say?" demanded Red Linny.

Persons smiled, perhaps the biggest smile that had ever crossed his face. "I hope you got a second set of eyes in the back of your head, 'cause you're gonna need 'em," said Persons. A single gunshot cut short his booming laughter, the smile still on his lips.

Moments later, the sound of all hell breaking loose erupted from upstairs.

Red Linny glanced at his watch. He had three more minutes before the time he'd purchased from the cops ran out. That meant someone else had shown up—the Calvary that arrived too late to save Knocks Persons.

The sounds of the firefight upstairs let him know that whoever had shown up wasn't fucking around. But neither was Red Linny. He'd brought four of his best soldiers with him—and by "best" that also meant expendable. His soldiers had dispersed throughout the house, taking out anyone keeping company with Knocks Persons, while he went downstairs to handle what needed to be handled. He'd left someone at the top of stairs—just in case—but he wanted to be alone for the killing. With no other witnesses, it would be up to every motherfucker in Harlem to fill in the blanks. By morning, niggers all over uptown would be talking about the murder of Knocks Persons, embellishing it with their own lurid details. Even the cause of death would be hotly contested. Old black men in barbershops would argue over whether or not Persons had been shot, or his throat slit. In the imagination of the streets, the corpse would be violated, the handiwork of a monster that had killed a monster.

Red Linny smiled at the thought of people thinking of him as a monster. He enjoyed that almost as much as feeling like God when dumb motherfuckers begged for their lives, not realizing they were already dead. And speaking of already being dead, whoever had shown up as last-minute reinforcements would be taken out as well. And if any of his soldiers were killed in the process, there would always be more bodies to put on the frontline. This was, after all, a war that Red Linny had declared. A war that he would win. It didn't matter who got killed in the process.

# EIGHT

Shaft couldn't believe how fast the shooter ran. For a cat in his mid-twenties, John Shaft felt he was in pretty good physical condition. The average person, however, would've considered Shaft a remarkable specimen of physicality. And yet, the shooter he pursued seemed to widen the gap between them with each stride.

The pursuer and the pursued respectively placed two and three blocks between themselves and the home of Knocks Persons before the police arrived at the scene of the crime. None of the responding officers noticed Shaft chasing after the gunman, who had veered off 138th Street on to Edgecombe Avenue.

Each home and building they passed seemed unusually dark and quiet, even for that ungodly time of morning. At the same time, Shaft knew that people were watching—peering out from behind drawn curtains, their lights off to avoid attention. By now, all of

fucking Harlem probably knew what had happened at
Knocks's place minutes earlier. That's how the streets
operated—a giant collective consciousness that knew
everything. There were already motherfuckers placing
bets on whether or not Shaft would catch the asshole
he was chasing. He knew this. Just like he knew people
were placing bets on whether or not one of them
would get killed. There were fuckers on the phone,
right now, offering play-by-play commentary as he ran
past. This is why he hated Harlem—it saw everything,
knew everything, and didn't give a good goddamn or
a holy shit about anyone.

The shooter turned right on to 137th Street, heading west. Shaft realized that his quarry was heading either toward the subway on St. Nicholas Avenue, or to
St. Nicholas Park. Either way, the chase would be over
at that point. The last surviving killer of Knocks Persons would get away if he reached the park or the subway.

The distance between Shaft and the shooter
widened. Shaft tried to aim his gun as best he could.
He hoped there were still bullets in it. He thought for
a moment about yelling out some type of warning, but

he could barely breathe as it was, and he really didn't give a shit about warning anyone. The gun came to life as he squeezed the trigger. The shot whizzed past the shooter, ricocheting off the concrete. Shaft cursed between gasps of breath, convincing himself that there'd been a time he would not have missed that shot, yet pleased that the runner had screeched to a halt.

Shaft slowed his pace to a quick jog, his legs and his lungs thanking him, as he closed the gap between himself and the shooter. The gunman that fled Persons's house stood in the middle of 137th Street, his hands in the air.

"Turn around slowly!" Shaft shouted from a distance that shrunk steadily. He held the gun in a two-handed, tactical grip, thinking that if it was out of bullets, he might be screwed.

Less than ten yards separating them, the shooter slowly turned around, hands in the air. An overhead streetlight bathed him in an unearthly glow, and for a moment, Shaft thought the shooter looked like an angel.

No, not an angel, thought Shaft. He's a kid.

There was no mistaking it—the killer that had fled the home of Knocks Persons was a kid. He couldn't be more than fifteen or sixteen at the oldest.

Shaft stopped dead in his tracks, a flood of memories washing over him like a tidal wave. First, he saw himself standing no more than five yards away, much younger, hands in the air—a memory of his own past. Then he saw an image that had been haunting him for the better part of a year—the dead body of a boy in a box—the taunting reminder of an unresolved case. And then that memory was pushed aside by the body of a Vietnamese teenager, dressed in black, his guts hanging out, splattered across jungle foliage in another part of the world, looking at Shaft with an expression that seemed to ask, "What the fuck did you do to me?"

Shaft aimed his gun at the teen boy standing in front of him. A million questions ran through his mind, but not a word left his mouth. Instead, he sized up the kid in front of him. The harsh glow of the streetlight created a stark contrast of shadows in the early morning darkness. The angle of the light illuminated the eyes of the boy, and Shaft could see it quite clearly—he was staring at a stone-cold killer. He'd seen eyes like that before—both in Vietnam, and growing up on the streets of Harlem. Shaft was sure, at one time or another, he'd had the same icy stare—he had too many notches on his gun belt to not have had that stare from time to time.

"Get it over with, old man," said the boy.

"What's your name?" asked Shaft.

"My name is Fuck You, Nigger."

"That's Mister Fuck You, Nigger," growled Shaft.

"Show some motherfuckin' respect."

"I got your respect right here between my legs. Why don't you come suck it, punk-ass faggot," said the kid.

"Who ordered you to take out Knocks Persons?"

"Yo' mama, right after I knocked the dust off her pussy."

"My mama, is dead, boy."

"Guess that explains why she's such a lousy fuck."

"We done playin' the dozens?" Shaft asked. "Either you talkin' to me, or you're talkin' to the cops."

"I ain't no rat," said the kid.

"No, you're just a dumb shit kid that just helped kill the Big Boss of Harlem."

At that, the kid smiled a sinister smile that sent a chill down Shaft's spine.

"There's a new boss, old man," sneered the kid. "Or ain't you heard?"

The roar of an engine and the screech of tires told Shaft that a car had turned on to 137th Street somewhere behind him. The fast approaching headlights racing toward his ass shone bright on the kid, whose sinister smile had turned into a laugh.

Shaft glanced over his shoulder, saw the oncoming car, and realized the driver had no intention of slowing down. Shaft pivoted, firing a gun that clicked empty. He made a mental note that maybe it was time he started carrying his own gun with him at all times, along with extra ammo.

The headlights of the car grew brighter as they grew closer, like the glowing eyes of a steel monster ready to devour John Shaft. Shaft leapt out of the way of oncoming car, but not quick enough to avoid his foot being smashed by the driver's side view mirror. The force of the blow spun Shaft mid-air, slamming him into a car parked at the curb, and knocking the wind out of him.

The car that nearly ran Shaft over screeched to halt inches from the kid, smoke from burnt rubber spitting from its tires. The kid walked over to the passenger side door, opened it and leaned in. He popped back out a moment later, gun in hand. He pointed it directly at Shaft. "Told you, old man," said the kid. "There's a new boss in town."

The kid popped off three quick rounds at Shaft, then hopped into the car. The driver took off before the kid had even closed the door.

Shaft sat on the cold concrete, his back leaning against the park car. He felt a burning pain. A familiar pain. One he'd felt more times than he liked to think about.

"Motherfucker," Shaft mumbled aloud. "That motherfuckin' kid just shot me."

# NINE

The bullet hit Shaft in what he decided to call his "lucky spot." He'd been shot in virtually the same spot once before, as well as catching a piece of shrapnel back in 1966. The piece of shrapnel, much like the two bullets, merely grazed him—entering and exiting his left bicep without shattering any bone or rupturing any major blood vessels. This most recent bullet would merely make a big scar a little bit bigger.

If he had a needle and thread, he could sew himself back together. It wouldn't be the first time he'd sutured himself and, he thought to himself, the way his life seemed to play out, it wouldn't be the last.

The wound burned, a familiar kind of fire, one he'd felt a few too many times for someone his age. On the other hand, he figured, not many people survived as many shootings, stabbings, explosions, and beatings as he had, and lived to tell about it. Hell, Shaft couldn't even think of anyone else who had a lucky spot like his—a place where they'd been shot twice, and felt the intense burn of shrapnel as it sliced like a hot knife through butter.

He chuckled to himself for a moment, almost forgetting where he was, what had happened, or what he'd left behind a few blocks away. *How far was it to Knocks Persons's place?* he asked himself.

It felt like he'd been running forever. And now, with the lingering rush of adrenaline, the burning pain in his arm, and the curious notion that no matter how many times he'd been shot, he'd always survived, John Shaft began to focus on the reality of the moment.

A few blocks away, Knocks Persons was likely dead. Shaft had no idea what condition Bamma Brooks might be in, though he had doubts as to whether or not the gangster was still drawing breath. Shaft didn't believe in much by way of God, or any sort of cosmic deity, but he did have a sense of life's bitter ironies. The fact that he and Bamma Brooks had walked into the same onslaught of hot lead, and that he was still alive, meant there was a good chance Brooks was dead. That was the bitter irony of life that Shaft had come to understand. It was the runaway bus that jumped the curb, and plowed into the poor sucker standing next to you. It was the apartment fire that started next door, but killed the neighbor down the hall. It was the sniper fire that turned the heads of the men immediately to your right and your left into a hot spray of warm, wet, red mist, but somehow missed you.

Shaft sat on the cold concrete pavement of 137th Street, leaning against the equally cold metal of a car parked at the curb. The only real warmth he felt was the steady trickle of blood coming from his arm. He didn't have to see the wound to know that it would need stitches—he knew what those wounds felt like. Six, seven stitches at the most would do the trick. First, however, he had to pick himself up, and head back the way he came, a thought that filled him with dread.

It wasn't finding Knocks Persons dead, or Cookie Venable's lifeless body, or even possibly Bamma Brooks that filled him with dread. No, there were two other things Shaft didn't want to face, waiting for him back at the killing field he'd just fled.

First, there would be the cops, which had no doubt arrived by now. Shaft didn't want to talk to them—to explain anything to them. He also knew that he ran the risk of them shooting him for a whole number of reasons, and that they might not hit his lucky spot, or any lucky spots, for that matter. The police would be in a heightened state of awareness once they arrived at the Persons's house that would translate to guns drawn, and an over eagerness to shoot at anyone black, which the NYPD never admitted to, but anyone browner than a paper bag new to be a fact.

The second thing that kept Shaft from wanting to return to the scene of the crime was the anonymous bodies that he knew were waiting for him. Not the guards of Knocks Persons, or whoever may have been unlucky enough to have stopped by for a late night social call—those bodies he was prepared to see. Or at least he was as prepared as he was ever going to be. No, it was the bodies of the other gunmen that John Shaft didn't want to see. He didn't want to know a single fucking thing about anyone he may have cut down as he fired into the darkness.

The face of the shooter that had fired three shots at Shaft, one of which hit him in his lucky spot, flashed through the private detective's mind. That little motherfucker couldn't have been more than fifteen or sixteen, Shaft thought to himself. He tried to focus on what the shooter's face had looked like, but instead recalled his own face—his own misspent youth. It was like the memory of looking at his own reflection as a teenager.

The last thing Shaft wanted to see when he got back to Persons's house—aside from some trigger-happy cops—was a bunch of dead teenage boys. That would be like looking down the road less traveled—the path he had avoided when the judge in the courtroom looked at him, and gave him the choice of prison or the military. Cookie Venable hadn't been given that choice, and he went down the well-worn path so many others had journeyed down—a twisting, turning trial of criminality. And now Cookie was dead. Just like so many others Shaft had known. Dead or in prison. He dreaded the thought of finding a house full of the former—the most recent generation of Cookie Venables, cut down and killed too young in their teens, as opposed to their mid-twenties.

Shaft felt a creeping melancholy that crawled up his back, and grabbed hold of him by the shoulders, whispering in his ear the familiar strains of the ghetto dirge that he'd heard his entire life. It was the lamentation of the poor and forgotten residents of crumbling inner cities and backwoods shit holes where life was cheap. It was a sad, old song when it was played for the father Shaft had never known—a numbers runner sliced and diced with a straight razor, and left to bleed to death in the street. It was the song playing at Knocks Persons's, dedicated to Cookie Venable, and whoever else may have fallen in the hail of bullets.

Shaft thought about all of this, and the kid who shot him, as he slowly walked back to Knocks's place. Somewhere, out there in the neighborhood he hated, there was a teenage kid who'd shot him. The sinking, sickening feeling that their paths might cross again left John Shaft hoping—fleetingly as it may have been—

that the cops waiting back at the home of Knocks Persons might become overzealous, and gun him down. It was an entirely unpleasant thought, but far more comforting than the possibility that he might square off against the teenage gunman again. He didn't know which was worse, getting killed by a younger version of himself, or him ridding the world of another killer. Killing a killer. That was another one of life's bitter ironies.

Fuck, Shaft thought to himself. I really hope the cops gun me down.

# TEN

"Yo, we need to go back," said Big Junior.

"Ain't no goin' back. Cops're probably there by now."

"But I don't know if I got that nigger or not, and he seen my face," Big Junior said.

The tires of the car screeched as Red Linny pulled a hard left on to St. Nicholas Avenue, heading south. He immediately slowed the car down, to avoid suspicion. "Then that shit is on you," said Red Linny, his voice, calm and cold, like a man incapable of caring about much of anything.

Big Junior pleaded, "But he seen my…"

Red Linny cut him off, "Motherfucker, shut yo' mouth, while you still have a face." His words came out with a steady calmness that made them a promise, more than a threat.

Big Junior held his tongue. He knew the price of crossing Red Linny, and he didn't feel like dying right there in the car.

Red Linny concentrated on the road, his mind racing, taking inventory of the last few minutes. Knocks Persons was dead, which meant the primary objective of the night had been met. He could still hear the sound of the gangster's booming laughter, cut short by a single bullet between the eyes. His dick had been so hard when he squeezed the trigger, and for a brief moment, he'd though about ramming it into the bullet hole and skull-fucking Persons. Not that he had ever done anything like that, or that such things turned him on, because he hadn't, and they didn't. But the thought of word spreading through the streets that he'd killed Knocks Persons, and then skull-fucked him? Well, that shit was exciting. That shit would make him a legend of the streets.

Unfortunately, there hadn't been anyone there to witness the violation in question, which would've made its commission some nasty-ass freak shit. Red Linny loved the idea of being thought of as a monster that skull-fucked his victims, but the actual sexual violation of any corpse held no interest for him. He didn't even care about fucking live bodies.

If there had been more time, he would've decapitated Knocks. He'd done the same thing to Willie Joe Pierce, and it had proved to be an effective way of scaring the hell out of everyone. Three weeks later, all of

Harlem wondered when and where Willie Joe's head would show up. There'd been a rumor that had started making the rounds that there were voodoo gangsters out of New Orleans that had taken the head, and that just made Red Linny laugh. And he'd overheard a conversation at Small's Paradise, in which he was certain he'd caught a sense of fear in Nicky Barnes's voice.

Had there been time for Red Linny to cut off the head of Knocks Persons, and then hide the motherfucker, people would lose their shit. Barnes and Lucas, and even Frank Marshall were all scared of Knocks—so scared they'd never dare to cross him outright—and Red Linny knew that everyone in Harlem would be living in fear of the Boogeyman that had killed the godfather and stolen his head. Damn, he wished he'd had more time to claim his prize. Instead, the fucking cavalry had shown up.

After the shooting had stopped, he'd barely had time to get out of the house, and make it to the car. Red Linny has passed the corpses of his soldiers—none of them over the age of sixteen. He felt nothing as he saw their dead bodies. Fuck it, they were all replaceable. He could get ten more before the sun rose, and another dozen by the time it set. The streets were filled with underage soldiers just looking to go to war, but they lacked a leader to send them into battle.

He didn't stop to see if Bamma Brooks was still

alive. Not that it mattered. With Persons dead, all bets were off. There would be a power struggle to control Harlem, mostly between Nicky Barnes and Frank Lucas—Frank Marshall was above all that shit, making him a different kind of threat. Brooks, and the handful of old school gangsters like him—those loyal to Knocks Persons, and Bumpy Johnson, who was dead, but still commanded loyalty—were not a problem. They'd die easy enough. Or take off out of town once the war started for real.

The biggest problem, or at least what Red Linny suspected the biggest problem might possibly be, had chased Big Junior out of the house and down the street.

Red Linny ran to the car that he had parked at the end of the block, and took off after whoever was chasing Big Junior. At first, he thought it might have been a cop, who hadn't gotten the word to stay away while business was being handled at Knocks Persons's home. He tried to run the motherfucker over, but the nigger had been fast—like Tommie Smith or John Carlos. The fleet-footed son of a bitch jumped out of the way of the car, and when Red Linny had stopped long enough to pick up Big Junior, he caught sight of the man he'd tried to run over. It was John Shaft—the last person he'd expected to see.

When Red Linny and his crew of teen assassins

stormed Persons's house, Cookie Venable had a look of shock on his face. Not shock over killers having come to the front door of his boss, but at the identity of the hit team's leader.

"Red?" asked Cookie, unbelieving, just before Red Linny shot him.

If there was any sense of loyalty or nostalgia connected to his past, Red Linny didn't feel it when Cookie Venable collapsed. Cookie Venable had been one of Red Linny's best friends, and watching him get shot didn't mean shit to Red. Their friendship had died long ago. Red couldn't say the same thing, however, when he saw Shaft. That brought a flood of emotions he thought he'd managed to burn out of existence; it rose like a phoenix from the ashes of the life he once led.

What the hell had Shaft been doing at Knocks's place?

"Red, man, shouldn't we be worried about that nigger back there?" asked Big Junior, breaking the silence of the last few minutes. Or maybe it had been the silence of a lifetime.

"The nigger's name is John Shaft," said Red Linny. He pulled the car over to the side of St. Nicholas Avenue, just past where it crossed 126th Street. "And you ain't got to worry about him."

Big Junior's face only had a fraction of a second to

register fear and shock before Red Linny blew his head off. Soldiers like Big Junior were easy to find, and easy to replace. But he would need better soldiers than that if he was going to go after John Shaft. He felt his dick getting hard at the thought of shooting Shaft through the head, and skull-fucking the corpse.

Red Linny got out of the car, leaving what remained of Big Junior's brains to spill out onto the vinyl upholstery. He limped to the nearest subway entrance, not giving a single thought to the loyal child soldier he had just killed. Instead, he thought about killing John Shaft.

# ELEVEN

Police detective Harry Townes spoke three languages fluently, not including English, and knew how to swear in another seven. He quietly cursed in eleven languages—including his native tongue of English, by way of the Bronx—as he pulled his car up to the cordoned off area surrounding the home of Knocks Persons. He combined the various expletives into a twelfth language of nothing but pure profanity, which he only used during the most special of occasions. The murder of one of the biggest gangsters in the history of New York qualified as just such an occasion.

Townes counted nearly a dozen police vehicles, both patrol cars and the unmarked rides of other detectives parked in front of the house a half block away. He wondered to himself who had caught the case, knowing full well that it was either O'Ryan or Kablonski. The mick or the Pollock, he thought to himself with disdain, two of the most corrupt cops working out of the Harlem precinct. If Townes were a betting man, he would've put down a month's pay that one or both of them were somehow in on the killing. The murder of Knocks Persons was a foregone conclusion—one he'd discussed with the gangster himself—and Harry Townes suspected that someone in the NYPD was in on the hit that was waiting to happen. The hit that had happened.

Everyone knew that the NYPD was riddled with corruption. In a police force marred with graft, bribery, brutality, and shakedowns that made the mob envious, New York's boys in blue were its most vicious gangsters—they had the law on their side.

Harry Townes was one of the most upright cops on the force, with a reputation that made him loved and hated with equal measure. His name, along with guys like Vic Anderozzi and Frank Serpico, was on the lips of every cop looking over their shoulder, afraid of getting busted for breaking the law. Not that he was a whistleblower like Serpico—who Harry openly admired—or even a hard-ass like Anderozzi. He was just straightforward, and incorruptible.

Word on the street had it that Bumpy Johnson once offered Harry Townes a bag with a million dollars in cash. In reality, it was Knocks Persons that made the offer, it had only been one hundred thousand dollars in the bag. One hundred grand to get

Townes on Persons's payroll as a top inside man on the force.

Harry figured it was the fact that he didn't take the money—he even tried to have Persons busted for attempted bribery—that the gangster actually trusted him. Their relationship was far too complicated to be considered a friendship, but they had history. Townes suspected that when the Moreletti crime family put a contract out on him, it was Knocks that stepped in and saved his life.

Townes got out of his car, and reached in his coat pocket for a pack of cigarettes, when he remembered that he'd quit smoking. Damn, he wanted a cigarette. And a drink. He could drink a toast to Knocks Persons, the best gangster he knew—except he'd quit drinking long before he gave up smoking.

One of the uniformed officers guarding the far outside perimeter of the crime scene gave Townes a knowing nod. Officer Les Mosely was one of the black officers stationed out of Harlem. There were more black officers in the Harlem precinct than any other in the city, but Townes still felt there weren't enough. As one of the few black detectives, he was a loud proponent for having cops in a community that closely resembled the residents. There were too many white cops stationed uptown that would be more at home walking a beat in some redneck stronghold in Alabama or Tennessee.

Every major race riot of the last ten years all seemed to spring from overzealous white cops beating the shit out of some black guy. Townes understood why so many people in the black community hated the police—he didn't much care for the cops himself, even if he was a member of the family.

"Who's on deck?" Townes asked.

"Koblanski caught this one," said Officer Mosely, a hint of contempt in his voice. "Motherfucker," said Townes. "Someone must really not want this one solved."

Mosely fought to keep from laughing—not because it was funny, but because it was true. Detective Stan Koblanski's reputation for corruption and brutality were equal only to his reputation for incompetence. Amongst cops that actually gave a shit about upholding the law, the common belief was that Koblanski was on the take simply to save up money for whenever someone woke up and realized he was a terrible cop, and fired his ass.

"Are you even supposed to be here?" asked Mosely. "I was just out picking up cigarettes."

"Thought you quit."

"Yeah, well I forgot that," said Townes.

Townes looked over at the giant house half way down the block. He would not be welcome at the actual crime scene—at least not by Koblanski. And probably not by anyone else on the force happy to see Persons finally knocked off his throne. There were too many cops that hated Persons, more because he was a wealthy and powerful black man, and less because he was the gatekeeper of vice and sin north of 96th Street. Townes, on the other hand, understood the bigger picture. For all the violence that plagued Harlem, Knocks was a ruler that kept the peace. His murder left a large hole of power that needed to be filled, and there would likely be a bloody war to see who had the biggest dick uptown.

"You hear anything about what happened inside?" asked Townes.

"Not much," answered Mosely. "Meat wagon is on the way—two of 'em. They won't let any of us close."

"Yeah, you might fuck up Koblanski's fucking up of the evidence," said Townes. "Damn. I wish I could get in there—just for a few minutes."

A voice came from behind them. "I'll make you deal—give me a ride, and I'll tell you everything I know."

Detective Harry Townes and Officer Les Mosely turned to see John Shaft. Both recognized him—it was hard not to. There had been enough newspaper and magazine articles that Shaft could be mistaken for a minor celebrity instead of a private detective. And there were those, like Mosely, that remembered Shaft from his brief, but legendary boxing career.

John Shaft had been the most promising amateur to come out of Harlem in years, and he'd thrown it all away during his first professional bout after refusing to take a dive.

Mosely hadn't been there that night at Prospect Gardens Sports Arena, but he'd heard the stories. Rumor had it that Shaft had actually knocked his opponent out of the ring.

Townes knew Shaft from more than his boxing career, and more than his work as a private dick, which had earned him a much-hated reputation within the force. Townes had never met Shaft, but he knew that Vic Anderozzi worked with him and, as much as he could, trusted the sleuth for hire. Unlike Anderozzi or Mosely, however, Harry Townes's knowledge of Shaft extended way beyond boxing or private detective work.

John Shaft had been the warlord of the street gang the Amsterdam Aces, better known as the Dam Aces.

Townes had been a uniform patrolman working Harlem, when he first heard of John Shaft, who couldn't have been more than fourteen or fifteen at the time. The Dam Aces were small in numbers, but big in reputation. They'd rumble with anyone, and often came out on top. Young John Shaft, warlord of the Dam

Aces, had a reputation that managed to work its way through Harlem like a modern-day folk tale. Word of his exploits had even crossed the river into the Bronx, where Townes's younger cousins lived, some of them bopping with the Bronx Brotherhood.

"John Shaft," said Harry Townes. As the name left his lips, he worried he sounded like someone meeting a celebrity, which, in his own way, Shaft could be considered.

"I know you?" Shaft asked. His mind was clouded, a jumbled mix of pain, crashing adrenaline, the lingering effects of too much Johnnie Walker Black, and something else he'd almost forgotten. In all the excitement of the gun battle, he'd nearly forgotten that just a few hours earlier he'd been balling some nameless chick that, for all he knew, was still sleeping in his bed.

"Harry Townes, NYPD," Townes said, extending his hand. That's when he noticed Shaft clutching his left bicep with his right hand, as a slow stream of blood trickled from what looked to be a gunshot wound.

"You working this case?" Shaft asked.

"Yes and no," answered Townes. "It's complicated."

Shaft looked over at the house a half block away. Uniformed cops, a few detectives, and paramedics— all of them white—hovered around like a cloud. None of them seemed to have any urgency, or purpose, or anything that looked to Shaft like they gave a shit about the dead and those possibly dying inside Knocks Persons's home. Not one to be poetic by any stretch of imagination, Shaft thought that the cloud outside Persons's home should be darker. Dark clouds indicated activity—that a storm was coming, or at the very least that the weather pattern was about to shift.

"I can't go back in there," Shaft said.

"Go back in?" asked Townes. "You were inside?"

"What the fuck do you think—that I cut myself shaving?" asked Shaft, indicating the wound on his left arm. "You want to know what I know, get me out of here, and I'll tell you everything. I just don't want to deal with them."

The way Shaft said 'them' hung in the air, dripping with disdain.

Without a word, Townes led Shaft back to his car. He stopped for a moment, and turned to face Mosely, who had remained silent the entire time. "Neither of us was here. That cool with you?"

Mosely looked at Townes. Then he looked at Shaft. Then he looked back at the house of the legendary Knocks Persons. Several of his fellow white officers were outside, smoking cigarettes and laughing about something. He wondered if any of them even remembered that he was standing there. He wondered if they cared.

"Never saw either of you," Mosely said.

Harry Townes opened the passenger side door for John Shaft, walked around the front of the car, got in, and started the engine. "Where to?" asked Townes.

# TWELVE

The bottom, left side drawer of the desk in Shaft's office contained the essentials.

There were bullets to a gun he'd misplaced, as well as a gun that had no bullets. The bottle of Johnnie Walker always seemed to be half-full, though he took pulls from it regularly, and couldn't recall ever replacing it. There was an unopened box of condoms, primarily because he rarely screwed any chicks in his office, and also because he seldom used the damn things. In the back of the drawer, tucked behind the empty packs of cigarettes, the half used books of matches, the packets of sugar that he habitually collected but never added to his coffee—because he hated his coffee sweet—there was a first aid kit.

Not just any first aid kit, this wasn't the kind you bought at the neighborhood pharmacy, or that Boy Scouts used to earn their merit badges. This was the real fucking deal—a military issue first aid kit. The kind guys in Special Forces and Long Range Recon carried in their just-what-you-need-to-survive ruck-sacks, when they were on solo missions deep in the jungle. This was the first aid kit of trained killers taught to survive on their own, in battle, without the back-up of a medic or a M.A.S.H. unit. It was for mean motherfuckers and tough sonsabitches that had the fortitude to stuff their own guts back inside them-selves, sew themselves up, and then hump their way out of the boonies.

Shaft had bought the kit from a Military surplus store on 8th Avenue—one of those places that sold mostly camping equipment, and was staffed by vets that either couldn't get work elsewhere, or simply didn't want to try that hard. For those in the know, the store simply named USA Army Navy Surplus, had a special showroom in the basement. You could buy anything short of a tank or an atomic bomb in the basement, and even then, you could get the phone number of someone who might be able supply you with one of the two.

Ricardo "Lefty" Lopez had been a Marine in Viet-nam when Shaft met him. Back then, he went by Ricky Lopez. After losing his left arm in a brutal firefight in the Mekong Delta, Ricky became ironically known as Lefty. One of his fellow Marines hooked him up with a job at USA Army Navy Surplus, and he had become something of an assistant manager for the black market operation in the basement.

Harry Townes watched in both wonder and a twinge of disgust, as Shaft cleaned out the wound on his left bicep, and then began to stitch himself together.

Shaft winced in pain as the needle first pierced one side of the wound, then the other, and he gently pulled the catgut thread tight, closing up his lucky spot. It took seven stitches, though he could've gotten by with six. By the time he started the third suture, he'd gotten so used to the pain he realized it made more sense to put in the final stitch, just for good measure, than to not.

"Give me a hand with this," Shaft said. "I need to tie off this last one, and I'm too fucking tired to do it myself."

Townes came around to the other side of Shaft's desk. He'd had his share of first aid experience back when he served in Korea, but he'd never seen anything—or anyone—quite like John Shaft.

"You've done this before?" asked Townes.

Shaft let out a chuckle, and lifted his shirt to show the many scars that covered his torso. He pointed to a relatively small, yet jagged scar, just to the left of his belly button. "That was the first time—1966. Doesn't look like much, but I swear to Christ my intestines were hanging out. Had to close myself up, and then take care of two others," said Shaft. "Our medic got his head blown off, and I was the only one in good enough shape to sew us back together."

Townes returned to his seat on the other side of Shaft's desk. Shaft put a bandage over his freshly closed wound, "Here's to not getting an infection," he said, holding up the bottle of Johnnie Walker, as if making a toast. He swigged the whisky, and then held the bottle out to Townes.

Townes shook his head. "Thanks, but no." "On the job?" asked Shaft.

"On the wagon," answered Townes.

Shafted nodded—neither an approval nor a condemnation—but merely an acknowledgement. He respected anyone who admitted to their problems, and faced them head-on. Someday, he might get around to doing that himself. But for now, he'd merely take another pull.

"Knocks Persons," said Shaft.

"Knocks Persons," said Townes. "He's probably dead."

"I'm going with definitely. It was like the fuckin' O.K. Corral up in Castle Persons. I don't think anyone got out of there alive," said Shaft.

"You got out."

"I got lucky," Shaft said. "I think Bamma Brooks

might not be as lucky."

Townes leaned forward in his seat—his curiosity piqued. "Bamma Brooks was there?" asked the cop.

"Brooks was the one who drove me over there," said Shaft. "Knocks sent him to get me. I tried to pull him to safety, but…" Shaft's sentence trailed off. Few things kicked at his soul like leaving a comrade-in-arms on the battlefield. Didn't matter if it was a fellow Marine, or a gangster in Harlem. Shaft had gone into battle with Bamma Brooks, and had likely left him to die on the cold marble floor. He took another hit of whisky, to quiet his conscious.

Harry Townes sat quietly, rolling the little bit that he knew around in his head. He wanted a cigarette almost as much as he wanted to grab hold of the bottle of Johnnie Walker, knowing that neither would sooth the feelings inside.

"Knocks Persons is dead. I'll be god damned," said Townes.

Shaft scrutinized Townes through heavy eyelids, weighed down by one too many swigs of whisky, and a long list of bullshit that added up to pure exhaustion. "I know," said Shaft. "I kind of liked Persons. As much as anyone can like a mean motherfucker like him."

"You gonna tell me what happened?" Townes asked.

"Not much to tell," Shaft said. He went on to explain the phone call that he'd received—the summons from the man himself—getting picked up by Bamma Brooks, and the massacre they wandered into.

"You're right, that's not much," said Townes. "Why would Knocks Persons call you, of all people?"

"Good question. Why were you at the scene of the crime? What the fuck? You out for a midnight stroll" Shaft glanced at his watch, "...two hours after midnight, and happen to saunter by Persons's place?"

"My relationship with Persons was..." Townes struggled to find the right word. "Complex."

This time, Shaft nodded his head. "Yeah, man, I understand complex. Can't tell you why he called me, but I'm guessing it had something do with our complexity."

"I heard about that job you did for him—where you rescued his daughter," said Townes.

The police detective referred to one of the more high profile cases of John Shaft's career. Persons hired Shaft to find his missing daughter, who had been kidnapped by Italian mobsters looking to take over the drug trade in Harlem. A bloodbath ensued.

"Not too many people that don't know about that case," said Shaft. Rescuing the estranged daughter of Knocks Persons, and the violence surrounding the case, had made the news, been the subject of a grand jury investigation, and made John Shaft more famous than he ever wanted to be. An article about the incident inspired a movie about him, which was still a sticking point, and the subject of a prolonged lawsuit against the producers. It also left people wondering why he didn't look like that pretty-boy model that had been cast as him, which really pissed him off. People would say, "You don't look like the guy in the movie," and he'd have to explain it as best as his lack of patience would allow.

Shaft and Townes sat in silence. Each man trying to make sense of his complex relationship with the man whose death promised to change the landscape of the city.

"Something happened to Knocks after that incident with Beatrice," said Townes. "His priorities changed. His view of himself changed."

"What the fuck, were you his shrink or something?" asked Shaft. "Or something," said Townes.

Shaft could see that the cop had something heavy on his mind. "Look, man, whatever it is you're holding back…let's just say that we don't need to play that game," said Shaft. "I just admitted to you my involvement in at least two deaths, and you haven't slapped the cuffs on me. I'm too tired for bullshit."

"Knocks tried to buy me off years ago, and I didn't bite. I think that made him respect me in a weird way," said Townes. He thought for a moment, choosing his next words carefully. "Persons shared certain information with me."

Shaft leaned forward in his seat, a look of disbelief on his face. "The fuck're you saying? That Knocks Persons was a snitch?" Shaft asked.

"No, not a snitch. Let's just say that he knew how to play this complicated game better than anyone else," said Townes. "I'm not naïve. I know the kind of man Knocks was—that he had people killed for less money than I make in a year. But he also knew when something subtler was needed. When his enemies needed to be taken down in a different way."

Shaft shook his head, laughing quietly. "Jesus H Christ, Knocks Persons fed the cops intel."

"Not the cops. Me," said Townes. "If he worked with anyone the way he worked with me, I don't know about it."

"You weren't kidding. That's one helluva complex relationship," said Shaft. "You don't know the half of it," said Townes. "Knocks Persons was working to clean up Harlem—he wanted heroin off the streets."

"Excuse me, it sound like you just said Knocks Persons wanted to get heroin out of Harlem," Shaft said, the disbelief in his voice cutting through the air.

"I know—hard to believe," Townes said, nodding his head. "That business with Beatrice changed him— I mean really changed him. He told me once that he couldn't live with himself knowing that when he died, he'd be leaving the world a worse place than when he came into it."

Shaft raised his bottle of whisky. "Here's to Knocks Persons and his existential awakening." He took another taste.

In his mind, Townes took a swig with Shaft. He wanted to take a drink to honor a man who didn't have much by way of honor, but who had come to a moment of clarity late in life. As an alcoholic, Harry Townes had had his own moment of clarity, and it only took his wife leaving for it to happen. For Persons, it had been the kidnapping of his daughter, watching her struggle to get clean, and realizing that he had created the world that almost destroyed her.

"Listen, Shaft, I can't prove it—and I have no idea who did it—but I know why Persons was murdered. I know it in my gut," said Townes. "Someone killed him because he had a plan. He never got into the details of it with me, but he told me he had it—he told me he was ready to make it happen. Knocks Persons was going to get heroin out of Harlem, and that's why he was killed."

# THIRTEEN

The death of Knocks Persons reverberated throughout the city, making front-page headlines, though with the *New York Times*, it was below the fold. The adjectives used to describe Persons varied from one news outlet to the other. All described him as a "Harlem businessman," while some used "alleged organized crime boss," and a few managed to sneak in words like "notorious," "ruthless," and "insidious."

The further one moved away from Harlem, the less his death was talked about on the streets. But in the kingdom over which he ruled, little else was discussed. Years earlier, Bumpy Johnson died of a heart attack, and that got everyone to talking. Knocks Persons getting gunned down in his own home made for even livelier conversations.

Compared to Bumpy Johnson's funeral, Knocks Persons's was somewhat subdued. If all of Harlem had shown up to bid farewell to the flamboyant Bumpy, only seventy-five percent showed by to say their good-byes to Knocks. Still, the who's who of uptown showed up, as did much of the who's who from further downtown. Crime bosses like Nicky Barnes and Frank Lucas showed up, in part to assuage rumors that one of them had put the hit out on Persons. Even Frank Marshall, who was out of town on one of his famous Las Vegas gambling trips, sent a bouquet of flowers that cost more than some people made in a month, while working overtime.

The underbosses that had been loyal to Knocks, and the soldiers that served beneath them, attended the funeral with a sense of palpable paranoia. Bamma Brooks, who survived the shootout, lay in a coma. His chances of survival were uncertain, but everyone knew he wasn't going to be at the funeral—not unless someone wheeled him into the church on a hospital bed and plugged in the machinery that kept his body alive while it decided whether it wanted to live or die.

Shaft read about the funeral and even caught a glimpse of the local news coverage as it played out on the television at the No Name Bar. Other than telling Harry Townes what had happened, no one else knew he'd been at the scene of the crime. He called Harlem Hospital to check up on Bamma Brooks, but refused to go in person. He had no way of knowing if Brooks's room was being watched by anyone other than the cops, who had him under twenty-four hour watch.

Aside from Brooks and Townes, there were two other people that knew John Shaft had been at Persons's house. First, there was the shooter—the teenager whose faced was burned into Shaft's memory. Second, was whoever had driven the car that nearly ran him down. The way Shaft figured it, whoever had been behind the wheel must have been in the house. If they had been outside, they could've come up behind both him and Brooks, and shot them in the back. No, there had been someone else in the house during the firefight. That person must've taken off out of the house after Shaft and the kid.

For nearly a full week, stories of Persons' death filled the news. Most of the facts, however, were omitted. None of the other victims were listed by name, though some reports mentioned that Persons had been killed along with "several others." There was a part of Shaft that ached to know exactly who those "several others" were. There were, of course, the gunmen Shaft had taken out. And though her name had been left out of all the stories, one of Knocks's mistresses had been unlucky enough to be in the house when the death squad came calling.

Nowhere had there any been mention of Clarence "Cookie" Venable. Shaft made a few discreet phone calls, pulled a favor or two, and made sure the funeral arrangements were made for Cookie. For all Shaft knew, Knocks may have had some sort of plan in place for Cookie and any other employees that met their maker, but that didn't mean shit to Shaft. He wanted to take care of Cookie's arrangements.

Much like Shaft, Cookie was an orphan, raised in boys' homes and foster care, and then on the rough-and-tumble streets of Harlem. Shaft had known Cookie longer than anyone else, with the exception of Ben Buford and Linwood Morton. But like those other childhood friends, he'd lost touch with Cookie, though there was a time when the two were like brothers. In fact, it was Cookie Venable that recruited Shaft into the Dam Aces, when John was all of twelve years old.

Shaft and Cookie had met in a foster home when they were both less than ten years old. They were re-united when John was twelve and Cookie was thirteen, and both were locked up in Spofford. Cookie had been big for his age, and strong, and had taken to protecting Linwood Morton, a tiny kid with a clubfoot. On the outside, they all ran with the Dam Aces. Ben Buford was part of the same gang, but he had a mother who cared about him, which meant he was never a hard-core thug like Shaft or Venable, or even Morton, who couldn't fight that well, but had more brains than all of them combined.

Had his life gone differently—had he never been

busted, or gone into the Marines, or done three tours of duty in Vietnam—Shaft had no doubts his life would've been different. Maybe he would've ended up dead, right next to Cookie Venable, soldiering for Knocks Persons.

Sitting at the bar at the No Name, slowly downing his favorite poison, John Shaft watched the muted television flash images of Knocks Persons's funeral. Shaft had come from Cookie's funeral at Pauper's Row, where no one else had shown up—just him, the gravediggers, and the priest who said a few empty to words to a God that either didn't listen, or didn't exist.

Shaft had thought about tracking down Ben Buford, to tell him about Cookie, and see if he'd want to go to the service. But the love/hate feelings Shaft had for Buford lacked the love part, and if he had to be honest with himself, he'd much rather it was Ben Buford being placed in the ground. He would've gladly skipped that funeral, even though he knew that was a lie. Ben's mother—the closest thing Shaft had to a mom of his own— would've asked him to go, and he would've done it. He would place his arms around the frail shoulders of Miss Maudie Buford, and console her as best he could over that sanctimonious cocksucker she called her son. Instead, he watched as two men he didn't know dumped dirt into the grave of a man he used to know.

Had he been paying more attention, Shaft might have noticed the other funeral service taking place on the other side of cemetery, where a sixteen year-old kid that he didn't know, but had shot dead, was being laid to rest. Shaft would have noticed that the only person at that service was the only other person that he wished was with him, mourning the death of his childhood friend. But John Shaft was too lost in his own world to see Linwood Morton, though the reverse was not the case.

Linwood Morton limped over to the other side of Pauper's Row, traversing the graves of the poor, forgotten, and the never-really-known. He watched from a safe distance as Cookie Venable was placed in the ground. He felt no remorse that he had been the one to shoot Cookie. In fact, the only thing Red Linny thought about, as he spied on that sorry excuse of a motherfucker named John Shaft, was how easy it would be to walk up and put a bullet through his skull. But that shit would be too easy. And it wouldn't be any fun.

# FOURTEEN

Other than making an appearance at Cookie Venable's sad excuse of a funeral service, John Shaft chose to lay low. His involvement in a multiple homicide hovered in the air, like a ghost trying to figure out the best way to haunt him. It might be hours, or it might be years, but sooner or later that ghost would be coming for John Shaft. If not in the form of the police—which seemed unlikely—then definitely in the form of whoever had taken out Knocks Persons.

Shaft spent most of his time at the No Name, his office pretending to do paperwork, or in his apartment, reading the note left behind by the last woman to warm his bed. "Thanks for a great time. Call me if you ever want to get together again," the note read.

She'd written down her number, but hadn't bothered to sign her name. She even drew little hearts instead of dots over the letter 'i'—but not her fucking name. Shaft didn't know what infuriated him most, and the fact that she hadn't personalized the note—hadn't made it out to him specifically, irritated him. He was convinced she didn't know his name either. Then he laughed, because if she had addressed the note to him, it would've been a "Dear John" letter, and that struck Shaft as funny.

He read the note over and over again—so many times that it started to become some sort of love sonnet. He went so far as to dial the first few numbers, before stopping himself. He didn't know her name—couldn't even remember if she was even that good in the sack—and yet he felt compelled to call her. He could ask her out, take her for dinner, maybe a movie, bring her back to the crib, and spread her legs, all the while pretending that he knew her name. He'd call her "baby," and maybe "sweetheart," and he'd let her get on top, and grind her hips until he felt the release that made him forget whatever he needed to forget. Right now, he needed to forget Cookie Venable. He needed to forget the teenager that shot him. And all he had to do was make a phone call and get some pussy, and he'd forget—if only for a brief moment.

*Jesus*, Shaft thought to himself, *how fucked up are you?*

Then he thought about calling Dr. Monica LaSalle, the psychiatrist. She could shrink his head for him. Or ball him. She'd been great in bed. She fucked with fury and rage, with all the resentment of a dutiful wife who had been betrayed by her husband. Her pussy was a weapon of revenge, and she knew how to use it. She'd screwed so hard she could make Shaft forget almost anything. And then she could talk to him about why he was so messed up in the head.

Shaft looked around his apartment. He felt the walls closing in, and the particular ghost that haunted his home was getting restless. This ghost, unlike all the others that haunted him, had nothing but his best interests at heart. And that's what made this spirit more difficult to contend with than any other. He could handle the dead Vietcong that haunted him in his sleep, and the other list of bodies that seemed to keep growing. Even the memory of Cookie Venable dying in front of him had become locked into his subconscious—burned into his memory. He knew it would be there forever. Yet the ghost of Cookie, and the Vietcong, and all the other bodies he dropped, didn't haunt him the way the one that resided in his apartment.

The memory of Arletha Havens, lying on the living room floor, murdered, was more vivid than the memory of the first time Shaft had kissed her. More vivid than the memory of her whispering in his ear, "I love you." More vivid than…

*Fuck. Snap out of it,* Shaft told himself.

At this rate, he'd end up getting drunk, and either looking for someone to fuck, or someone to kill.

He picked up the phone, called his answering service, and prayed that Mildred would answer. Mildred was the only operator at the We Never Sleep So You Can Answering Service that he liked talking to on the phone. Shaft had never met her face-to- face, but he knew more about Mildred and her life than just about anyone else he knew. He knew it was pathetic that some of his best friends were Vic Anderozzi, a cop that only half trusted him, and Mildred, last name unknown, an operator at his answering service.

"We Never Sleep So You Can Answering Service," said the voice on the other end. It did not belong to Mildred.

"This is John Shaft…"

"Hold on a moment, Mr. Shaft," the operator said, cutting him off. "Let me get Mildred for you."

Shaft held the line, and looked at his watch. He realized that he'd called during the shift change. Mildred shouldn't even be there at this hour.

"Mr. Shaft, is that you?" asked Mildred.

"Mildred, what are you doing working so late?" asked Shaft. "Oh, it's Emil," said Mildred.

Emil, Mildred's husband, felt like an old friend John Shaft had never met. Shaft knew all about Emil, including how Mildred was convinced he was having an affair, even though he was well into his sixties, and seldom left the apartment. "What's wrong with Emil?" Shaft asked, worried that the old man's high blood pressure might be acting up again.

"Nothing to worry about, Mr. Shaft," Mildred said. "He had to go out of town to visit his brother, and I refused to go. His brother is an a-s-s-h-o-l-e. You know, he once pinched me on the bottom."

"I know, you told me about that. And you slapped him and threatened to cut off his fingers."

"I most certainly did," said Mildred. "I am a respectable woman, Mr. Shaft. Not some floozy."

Shaft smiled, almost laughing at the thought of the woman, whose face only existed as a conjured abstraction in his imagination, threatening to cut of the fingers of her lecherous brother-in-law. Part of him desperately wanted to meet Mildred and Emil in person, though he suspected his relationship with the older couple could never be better than it was as it existed—with her as a disembodied voice, and him as a supporting character in her story. For all Shaft knew, Emil might not even really exist—he might be a manifestation of poor Mildred's loneliness. Maybe Mildred was like Jimmy Stewart in that movie about the guy with the invisible rabbit for a best friend, and all the other operators at the We Never Sleep So You Can Answering Service just humored the crazy old broad whenever she talked about him.

"Well, Emil is out of town for a few days," continued Mildred, "and I hate being alone, so I decided to work some extra shifts."

*She hates being alone*, Shaft said to himself. That added proof to his theory that Mildred made up Emil, like Jimmy Stewart made up the rabbit. Damn, Shaft couldn't remember the name of the rabbit. And he hadn't even screwed the rabbit.

"Any messages?" Shaft asked. Not that he really cared. He just needed to distract his mind from any more ridiculous wandering—it's why he called to check his messages in the first place. He didn't give a shit if anyone had called him, he just needed a break from what he suspected might be his own diminishing sanity.

"Just the usual the stuff, Mr. Shaft. Although there was one man who's called several times, and his message didn't make much sense."

"How so?"

"Not to get into you personal life, or anything like that," said Mildred—even though she regularly tried to get into Shaft's personal life. "But I thought you didn't have any family."

"That's right," said Shaft. Orphaned at an early age, with no siblings, the closest thing to family John Shaft had were ghosts like Cookie Venable, and assholes like

Ben Buford.

"Well, this man—the one that called several times—he says he needs to talk to you about your inheritance."

# FIFTEEN

Shaft couldn't shake the feeling that he either needed a gun to go with the bullets in his bottom left desk drawer, or bullets to go with the gun. He made a trip to see Lefty Lopez, confident he could get one or the other from the 'Nam vet. It made more fiscal sense to buy bullets for the .45 automatic, than to invest in a .38, especially since he didn't care for the latter.

With the exception of the .45 he kept in his desk drawer, and the guns he kept hidden around his apartment, where they only seemed to gather dust, Shaft had trouble holding on to firearms. It seemed like most of the guns he used were taken from someone pointing one at him—a trick at which he was especially adept. In fact, if there were a black belt in disarming a motherfucker pointing a gun at you, and then using it to kill the sorry sonovabitch, Shaft would have one those black belts. But he never held on to those guns for too long, and he realized that it was the closest thing to a superstition he had.

Other people didn't walk under ladders, or freaked out when a black cat crossed their path. That shit seemed irrational. But getting rid of a gun you just snatched from someone, and then using it to kill them? That was good goddamn sense.

Lefty gave Shaft the bullets and an extra magazine for free. He owed Shaft for some past work the detective had done for him, though Shaft was more than sure the debt had been repaid. Shaft tried to hand Lefty a roll of cash, and the Lopez pushed it away with his remaining hand.

"You don't owe me anything," said Shaft.

"I owe you everything, Johnny," said Lefty. "My entire family owes you."

Shaft nodded his head without saying another word. Some things didn't need to be said, part of an unspoken language only understood by soldiers in combat, or anyone bonded by the mutual experience of killing. Shaft and Lefty understood the language in its many dialects. They spoke it fluently as veterans of the conflict in Vietnam, but they also understood it in the particular parlance of uptown, where both had fought in different kinds of wars. Shaft had done work for Lefty and his family, not so much as a detective, but more as a fellow bastard child of war, and a soul brother of the streets.

Shaft left the USA Army Navy Surplus store, walking north along 8th Avenue, toward his office. He had more than enough time before his meeting, and he preferred walking to taking the subway. On 42nd Street, he headed east for two blocks, taking in the sights and sounds of the freaks, transients, and denizens that inhabited the area surrounding the Port Authority bus terminal and Times Square. Part of him loved this part of the city, if for no other reason that its total lack of pretense. Here, more than anywhere in the city, maybe even the world, bat-shit-fucking-crazy was perfectly normal.

Insanity existed everywhere, as people stumbled around blindly grasping for whatever remained of their humanity, trying to steal it from others, shoot it into their arms, or fuck it back into existence. The entire world was an insane asylum, where the inmates tried to act sane. But there was no hiding behind the façade of sanity or normal civil behavior in this part of the city.

In one block, you could see a drunken bum, squatting on the corner taking a shit, a transvestite giving a businessman a blowjob in a phone booth, and some wild-eyed preacher asking if you'd found Jesus. And it was all normal. Or at least no one tried to pretend like it wasn't normal. If there were a difference, he didn't think about such things. Instead, Shaft just made it a point to avoid stepping in the pile of shit that he was pretty sure had been deposited by the bearded man, babbling to himself, wandering down 42$^{nd}$ Street, pants still down around his ankles.

Shaft knew other people that avoided this part of the city the same way he avoided Harlem. But he felt comforted by the insanity that he managed to avoid stepping in, kept at arm's length, and never let sneak up behind him. This insanity, of people who had lost touch with their humanity, and existed like feral animals in a forest of concrete and steel, made John Shaft feel a little less crazy. Here, in this neighborhood in which reason had long since packed up and moved to the suburbs, Shaft had found the perfect stick to measure his own sanity. As long as this place existed, and it was over-run by these people, he knew he wasn't that crazy. Crazy, yes. But not that crazy.

Shaft arrived at his office two hours before his scheduled meeting. This gave him plenty of time to check the various spots where someone might lie in wait, hoping to catch him unaware. Others had tried to ambush him in the various spots surrounding his office that provided the best tactical advantage, but they had all failed. Some had failed at the cost of their lives. Aside from knowing the area that bordered his office, he had eyes everywhere—people looking out for him who, for the cost of a five-dollar bill, would tip him off to potential trouble.

Fairly certain that he wasn't in any immediate danger, Shaft made his way up to his third floor, single-room office that overlooked Times Square. Mildred had given him the number of the man who called about some kind of inheritance. The number belonged to Abraham Scher, attorney at law.

Shaft had no recollection of ever meeting an Abraham Scher, and though he had no reason to be paranoid, a certain amount of paranoia had kept him alive this long, so there was no reason to stop. He'd set up a meeting with Scher, get to his office early enough to scope out the area, load his .45, and slowly sip his cup of black, unsweetened coffee.

Shaft tossed two packets of sugar into his bottom desk drawer, and wondered why he always took two packs that he never used. If he ever got around to getting his head shrunk, maybe he could talk about that. Hoarding packets of sugar that he never used would have to be easier than talking about the forgotten names of the unknown number of women he'd bedded. Or, he could just go for a walk in Times Square, and remind himself that no mater how fucked up he may be, he wasn't taking a shit on the sidewalk while talking to himself.

Waiting for Scher, Shaft absent-mindedly picked up his well-worn copy of *Manchild in the Promised*

*Land*, and started reading it for what must have been the tenth time. Arletha had given him the book and it was the only reading material he kept at the office, other than the newspapers he picked up at the corner newsstand, or the occasional issue of *Playboy*.

The knock on his office door came a few minutes before the meeting was to start.

Shaft checked his gun, made sure there was a round in the chamber, the safety was off, and the weapon could be reached with ease.

"Come in," said Shaft.

The door opened, and an older white man—in his sixties, if not his seventies— entered carrying a cardboard box. Nothing seemed threatening about the man, but Shaft cast a quick glance at his gun. If this old motherfucker tried anything, Shaft would blow him away without a second thought.

The old man set the box down on the floor with a soft thud. "Mr. Shaft," said the old man, offering his hand across the desk, "I'm Abraham Scher—like Sonny and Cher."

Shaft rose from his seat, and took the old man's hand. His grip was firm— especially for someone who looked so frail—and it reminded Shaft of the dangers of judging a book by its cover. For all Shaft knew, Scher might actually be one of those highly trained Israeli assassins, like the ones he'd tangled with not that long ago. Those Jewish cats were some of the meanest motherfuckers he'd ever tangled with, and Shaft worried that the gun he had close at hand might not be close enough.

"Please, have a seat," said Shaft. "Now, what can I do for you?"

Abraham Scher smiled, and patted the top of the cardboard box. "I bring all that has been bequeathed to you by my client," said the lawyer.

Shaft looked at Scher with uncertainty. "Exactly who is your client?" asked Shaft.

The change in Scher's expression was subtle, but noticeable. His smile had not turned completely into a frown, but it had come close. Without knowing the man, Shaft could see the emotional shift in Scher, like a subtle breeze that only registered by the way it moved the leaves on a tree.

Scher let out the tired sigh of a man who held in too many secrets. "My client— my dear friend—was Knocks Persons," said Scher. He tapped his finger on the top of the box. "And he wanted you to have this in the event of his death."

# SIXTEEN

Abraham Scher began to weep uncontrollably. His chest heaved, his body wracked, and tears streamed from his eyes in a display of emotion that made John Shaft uncomfortable.

Shaft reached for the box of tissues he kept on top of his desk. He discovered long ago that one of the most important tools a private detective could use was a box of tissues. He'd worked enough divorce cases—spying on husbands and wives suspected of cheating by their partner—that he'd come to expect the tears. He seldom left his office with a gun, but his office was never empty of a box of tissues, the only comfort he could provide after shattering the illusion of marital bliss, and before presenting his bill.

Shaft had seen plenty of emotional displays in his life. He'd even had a few himself. There had been that time, in Vietnam, when he was still a cherry, and he held his best friend close while the man died. For the life of him, Shaft couldn't remember the man's real name—only his nickname, Tricky. He could still feel the short, rapid breaths of Tricky—still feel his slowing heartbeat. Shaft could still hear Tricky, crying, asking for his mother, begging himself not to die, as if he had any say in the matter.

After Tricky died, Shaft lost it. He'd never experienced anything like that before, and felt certain that when he returned from that place of raging emotions, he wasn't the same person. Holding another man as he dies changes everything. Having to go out the next day and kill changes everything even more. The tears come less frequently. The emotion becomes an inconvenience that gets in the way of what needs to be done.

Shaft felt an equal mix of envy and pity for people like Abraham Scher—people who could still feel something as deeply as they did. It had been a long time since Shaft had ever felt anything that deeply, and it had not brought forth an emotional display like the one he was witnessing. No, the death of Arletha Havens had merely pushed him into a deeper, darker hole, where everything felt number, and the killing came more easily.

Abraham Scher took the box of tissues offered by Shaft. "My apologies, Mr. Shaft," said Scher, wiping the tears from his eyes. "I thought the worst of this had passed."

"It's okay," said Shaft. He didn't know what else to say. In his wildest dreams, he would never have imagined the old Jewish man sitting across from him, mourning the death of Knocks Persons.

"No, Mr. Shaft. You do not understand. My guardian angel is dead."

It took all he had for Shaft to not give his are-you-a-crazy-motherfucker look to the old Jew. Knocks Persons was many things to many people, but a guardian angel was not one of them.

Scher pulled up the sleeve of his finely tailored business suite, removed the cufflinks from his shirt, and rolled up his sleeve, revealing a series of numbers tattooed on his forearm. "I was a young man when I was brought to the camp—still very much a boy in so many ways," Scher said. "I had been a petty thief—a pickpocket—and in time, I came to believe my being there was punishment from God. I prayed. I begged God to deliver me, promising him that I would change my life."

Scher close his eyes, wiping away tears that showed no sign of stopping. "Have you ever seen pictures of camp survivors, Mr. Shaft?"

Shaft nodded his head. He had seen the pictures. Men and women that looked like skeletons—more dead than alive—starved and tortured and left to die as evidence of the evil other men can do.

"Then you can imagine what I must have looked like," said Scher. "I weighed less than one hundred pounds. All of my hair had fallen out. I could not stand, let alone walk. I was covered in the waste of others, and perhaps most important, Mr. Shaft, I had stopped believing in God. He had not answered my prayers. He did not believe my promise of turning my life around. And then God sent unto me an angel. A giant, black mountain of a man, that picked me up and carried me off. The man spoke to me in broken German, saying, 'Alles wird gut.' Everything will be fine. That man was Knocks Persons."

Shaft fancied himself a man of few words, though seldom did he feel at a loss for them. There were, however, no words that came to mind as he sat across from the sobbing Scher. All Shaft could really think about was how little he knew of Knocks Persons. He had met the man, interacted with the man, and even grown up hearing the stories—the tall tales spoken up and down the streets of Harlem. In all the stories he'd heard, there were none that involved the gangster serving in World War II. No one had ever spoken of Knocks being present at the liberation of Buchenwald, or Dachau, or whatever living hell Scher had endured.

Shaft realized that for all he knew about Knocks Persons, he knew very little. And to see the old Jewish man, crying over Persons, who he thought of as his guardian angel, it dawned on Shaft that he knew even less than he'd thought. He tried to picture Persons, twenty-five years younger, in the uniform of the 761st Tank Battalion—the true Black Panthers—stealing the much younger Scher away from the immediate grasp of the Grim Reaper.

Scher fought to compose himself, as Shaft wondered if there was anyone who would mourn his passing with such raw emotion. One of the many women whose names he couldn't remember? The guys down at the shoeshine stand around the corner from his office? Mildred?

He doubted any of them would shed tears the way Scher shed them over Persons, and it caused Shaft to look at the life he'd led thus far. Somewhere, on the other side of the world, there were people in Vietnam, that didn't know him, had never met him, but would no doubt be elated to know of his death, if they only knew he had been the one to kill their fathers and brothers and husbands.

"Again, Mr. Shaft, I am sorry for this display of emotions," said Scher.

Shaft tried to think of what the old man must be feeling. Somewhere, deep inside, he felt a glimmer of something he didn't quite understand, though it felt to him like relief. He felt that if anyone could mourn the passing of someone like Knocks Persons with such unrestrained emotion, then maybe, just maybe, there was still a chance he could get his shit together, and become a better person.

*Maybe, if I'm lucky, someone will cry like this over me someday*, Shaft thought to himself.

"I'm sorry for your loss," said Shaft. He meant it, feeling a twinge of his own personal loss over the Knocks Person he never knew.

"I don't expect you to fully understand my grief," said Scher, showing signs of finally pulling himself together. "I know the kind of man Knocks was—what he was capable of doing. But when you have survived the most evil of atrocities, a man like Knocks does not seem quite so bad."

"No, I don't suppose he would," said Shaft. He thought of his own actions, carried out in service to the United States Marine Corps—actions that could be viewed as evil atrocities, depending on your perspective. Shaft had never gassed any Jews, but he sure as fuck had helped to reduce the population of Northern Vietnamese. If he believed in Heaven and Hell—really, truly believed—John Shaft knew exactly where he'd be going. Maybe Knocks Persons would be saving a place for him at the table, along with all the other motherfuckers who did what they did, while the world around them suffered.

Shaft grew tired of the endless flood of thoughts

tearing through his mind like a tornado determined to level all in its path. Too much had happened over too short a period of time for him to be caught in one of those goddamn existential conundrums over the nature of good versus evil, right versus wrong, and on which side of the line he stood. He very much wanted Scher to pick his Jewish ass up off the chair, and stroll out of Shaft's life, so the private detective could go back to pretending he didn't give a shit about the tug of war raging in his soul.

There was a bottle of Johnnie Walker calling out to him, and the phone number of a woman with no name, but two legs that could spread perfectly. Shaft could retreat to both, not give another thought to Knocks Persons, or all the dead Viet Cong, and simply call it day.

But there was the box, sitting on the floor, next to Scher, who seemed to stroke it like it were a pet dog. Shaft had no clue what the box contained, nor was he sure he wanted to know. There might not be enough whiskey or pussy to deal with the contents. For a man that feared nothing outside of what was in his own mind, Shaft eyeballed the box with a certain amount of dread. He couldn't imagine anything that Knocks Persons could bequeath to him that would be any different than a box given to him by a broad named Pandora.

"What's in the box?" Shaft asked.

Abraham Scher looked down at the box. "This box contains the most dangerous thing Knocks Persons ever had," said Scher. "It contains the truth, Mr. Shaft."

# SEVENTEEN

"What about Bamma Brooks?" asked Red Linny Morton.

"What about him? I'm not the one who left him lying there, still breathing. That's your fuck up, not mine."

Red Linny stared at the aging white man across from him with a cold indifference that hung in the air like a thick fog. Detective Stan Koblanski pretended as if he wasn't intimidated by the killer that was more than thirty years his junior. In reality, however, Morton scared the shit out of Koblanski.

To look at him, there was nothing remotely frightening about Linwood Morton. He stood just over five feet, eight inches tall, and couldn't have weighed more than a buck-fifty. He walked with a limp that betrayed one leg as being more than a full inch shorter than the other. His hi-yella skin tone almost made him look white, except that his strong Negro features revealed the truth. His full lips and broad, flat nose seemed out of place on someone with such a light complexion. Atop his head sat a close-cropped, kinky red afro. He almost looked like some kind of clown, his appearance made all the more odd by heterochromia, the genetic anomaly that made Red Linny's eye color mismatched—one sky blue, the other a dark, murky brown, and both devoid of anything resembling compassion or pity. Koblanski thought Morton's eyes looked weird, but he knew that others took the coloring to be something significant.

Everything about Red Linny's appearance left Koblanski feeling unsettled. His actions, however, were what really scared the cop. Koblanski had known some cold-blooded sociopaths in his day, but Red Linny made them all look like average joes just having a bad day. Those that knew of Red Linny spoke about him more like a boogey man than a gangster. Some of his crew consisted of Haitian refugees, exiled from their homeland by dictator Papa Doc Duvalier or, more recently, his son Baby Doc. Koblanski knew that the Haitians that worked for Morton held him in some quasi-godlike regard that he figured had to do with those damn creepy eyes. Koblanski imagined Red Linny and his Haitian henchmen sitting around the dinner table, eating the hearts of their enemies and raping white women—or whatever it was crazy voodoo spades did in their free time.

Among the most notorious traits of Morton was his propensity for employing kids, and showing no regard for them at all. Rumor had it that Red Linny bought Haitian children from some ex-Tonton Macoute—the secret police of Haiti—that had set up shop in Florida, peddling young flesh, cocaine, and guns. Koblanski didn't know if it was true or not, but he did know for sure about the other kids. Morton had a deal going with someone in the city's foster care system— a deal that made even someone as corrupt as Koblanski sick to his stomach. There were at least a dozen unsolved homicides of minors in Harlem, and Koblanski was willing to bet a year's salary all of them had worked for Red Linny. Hell, the psychopath had killed one of his own after getting away clean from Knocks Persons's house.

"If I was worried about Brooks, I'd walk into the hospital and kill the motherfucker myself," said Red Linny. "That's not why I'm askin' about him. I'm askin' 'cause I want to know who's come to see him."

"Who cares who's coming to see him?" Koblanski asked.

"I care. Brooks was one of the last ones loyal to Persons and, by my reckoning, the next in line to take control of Harlem," said Red Linny. "Anyone checking on Brooks is still loyal to Persons, and those fuckers need to be eliminated. That's my job. You understand that?"

Koblanski understood as well as anyone what the death of Knocks Persons meant. A power void now existed in Harlem, and someone would need to step up and take control. Bamma Brooks was the last powerful player from an era quickly fading from memory. Koblanski had worked uptown for so long, he knew all the players—he'd taken pay-offs from all of them, big and small. And he knew that the fate of Harlem rested in whoever stepped up to take control of the empire Red Linny had destroyed with a bullet to the brain of Knocks Persons. Not that Koblanski gave a shit about any of the spades running around, slicing each other with switchblades. All he cared about was making money.

"We've got an officer outside of Brooks's room 'round the clock," said Koblanski. "Every last one of 'em is with me. No one has been to see that dumb sap."

"That's too bad," said Red Linny. "Motherfucker like Bamma Brooks—big bad nigger runnin' a crew of his own—you'd think someone would care enough to visit his ass. Bring him some flowers or some shit like that."

Koblanski couldn't tell if Linny was being serious or not. The red-headed gangster, with the pale complexion and the mismatched eyes was impossible to read.

"Though I suppose, if it was my yella ass up in that bed, wouldn't no one come see me either," Linny said. He looked around at the crew of bodyguards that surrounded him, none of them over eighteen. Everyone would kill for him, but he doubted any would ever come visit him in the hospital.

Linny reached into the inside breast pocket of his jacket. Koblanski's heart skipped a beat, and he caught himself as he reached for his service weapon, the click-clack sound of guns being cocked letting him know he was stepping out of line.

Red Linny laughed—a dangerous and deadly chuckle as much a sign of amusement as some kind of warning. It was his way of saying that the detective didn't need to worry about dying right that very moment, as long as he knew his place.

"No need for all of that," said Red Linny. He waved one of his hands, signaling to his bodyguards to holster their weapons. He fought to keep from smiling, even though the thought of anyone of those kids blasting a hole through Koblanski made him giddy.

From inside his jacket, Linny produced a wad of cash, two inches thick, bound together by a couple of thick rubber bands. He tossed the money to Koblanski, who caught the bundle of one hundred dollar bills.

"That's for you and your boss, from me and my

boss," said Red Linny.

Koblanski didn't count the money. Not that he trusted Red Linny. He didn't trust anyone, especially not albino-looking spade criminals with mismatched eyes. But counting the money would've shown his lack of trust, and that would've just made things more tense. The way Koblanski figured it, if he'd been shorted, he'd find a way to make things right. He was, after all, a cop. And cops like him knew how to make things right, without ever getting caught.

Koblanski pocketed the money—more than he made in a year, including overtime. "I'll let you know if there's any news about Brooks," said the corrupt cop.

"Good," said Red Linny. "I hear-tell Barnes has got a big shipment of coming in. Looks like his connections with Crazy Joe Gallo are finally paying off."

"Yeah, I heard something about that."

"Make sure you tell your friends in narcotics to let that shit hit the streets," said Red Linny. "Let it all hit the streets, no matter who's movin' the product. Don't care if it's them southern niggers, or Fleetwood King's crew 'cross the river in the Bronx. Make sure it all gets on the streets."

"You got it," said Stan Koblanski. He hated taking orders from anyone, especially someone like Morton. It didn't matter that Red Linny practically looked white—he was a darkie just like all the others. A powerful darkie—working for someone higher up the food chain than Koblanski was used to dealing with—but a darkie none-the-less.

Koblanski stood to leave, but before he could move, Red Linny stopped him. "One last thing," said the gangster. "What you know 'bout John Shaft?"

"That private dick, operates outta mid-town?" asked Koblanski.

"Yeah. That's the one. He been snooping around on this thing?"

"Not that I know of," said Koblanski.

Red Linny nodded for a moment, trying to decide how much Koblanski needed to know—like the fact that Shaft had been at Persons's house the night of the killing. Koblanski not knowing anything about Shaft didn't mean shit, other than the fact that he was a half-ass police officer who made more money looking the other way than he'd ever made actually doing cop work. Red Linny looked forward to the day when he got the go-ahead to rid the world of Stan Koblanski. He might actually get around to finally skull-fucking someone on that day.

"Keep an eye open for Shaft," said Red Linny. "Someone's gonna have to kill that motherfucker sooner or later. Most likely sooner. Might as well get that set up."

# EIGHTEEN

Like most cops, Harry Townes hated doing stake-outs. He hated them even more now that he'd quit smoking. The fact that he'd only been on this particular stakeout for under an hour didn't mean a damn thing. He wasn't officially on duty, and he couldn't smoke, which made everything a special kind of hell. He sipped on the worst cup of coffee he'd ever tasted, staring down the street at what should've been an abandoned building—one of those condemned deals that littered Harlem, and made it look like a desolate wasteland.

From his vantage point, Townes identified what had to be six spotters, strategically placed in the area immediately surrounding the boarded up four-story apartment building. He made a note to check with someone he trusted in the narcotics division—maybe this was a shooting gallery, or maybe one of those processing factories that were popping up all over. Townes couldn't be sure. All he knew was that Koblanski had gone inside a building that, in theory, wasn't occupied.

Townes could see faint glimmers of light peeking out from between the plywood planks nailed over the windows. He couldn't see where someone had run a line from a nearby streetlamp to supply electricity to the building, but he knew it was there, bringing light and life to a building that was supposed to be dead. Harlem and the Bronx were filled with buildings just like this, condemned properties, left for dead, resurrected by someone within enough savvy to known how to steal power from the city. Buildings like this made Townes think of Frankenstein's Monster—something dead, brought back to life. He used to watch all those old monster movies on Channel Nine, and now they reminded him of the lives he saw on the streets. Even as a kid, Townes identified with the monsters. As a black kid, in America, if was difficult not to identify with the monsters—those tragic freaks like the Wolfman, or the creature made by Dr. Frankenstein—who didn't ask to be what they were.

In the week since Knocks Persons had been killed, there had been no leads in the case. Not that it surprised Townes—Koblanski's reputation of being a bad cop had doomed the case from the beginning. At the very least, Townes had figured that Koblanski would do a half-ass job, but through some sneaking around, asking a few questions here and there, it had become clear that the corrupt cop was doing less than a half-ass job. In fact, given that there were no suspects in the killing, it could be said that Stan Koblanski was doing a no-ass job.

Bamma Brooks lay in a coma over in Harlem Hospital, and all of uptown had started to fall apart. Moves were being made by every player—some cautiously, some with a brazen audacity that showed who was vying to be the top dog. More heroin had hit the streets in the past week than over the last several months—a sure sign that without Knocks Persons clamping down on the influx of dope, a flood would soon hit Harlem. There were already rumors that Nicky Barnes had set up a major buy through his Italian contacts. And over in the Bronx, word had it that Fleetwood King had at least ten kilos of uncut smack, and was ready to set up shop in Harlem. Townes figured that the ten kilos was probably no more than a single key, and that was only if Fleetwood King had gotten a really good hook up.

Bodies had already started to drop, which meant a turf war was brewing. Hell, for all Townes knew, it already started. He feared that the killing of Knocks Persons would be for Harlem what the assassination of Archduke Franz Ferdinand had been for Europe—the start of a long and bloody war.

Townes checked his watch. Koblanski had only been in the building for a short time, but without any cigarettes, it felt like an eternity. Townes had been tailing the other detective as much as he could for three days, the results proving to be fruitless. If Townes had been out gathering intel for the Knapp Commission or some shit like that, he'd have a ton of dirt on Koblanski. Not that the Knapp Commission had done much of anything other than make a bunch of headlines, get the general public riled up, and make Frank Serpico the most well-known cop on the force. At the end of the day, cops like Koblanski kept right on doing their same old shit. A few of them looked over their shoulders a bit more, took a few more precautions as they waded up to their necks in water filled with graft and corruption.

Stan Koblanski didn't even bother to look over his shoulder. He operated with either a complete disregard for anything resembling discretion, or as a complete fucking moron. Townes couldn't be sure which it was, though he suspected the latter. Over the course of three days of his extra curricular tailing of Koblanski, Townes had seen him take possession of no less than three pay-offs, act as the drop-man twice, and get a blowjob from a hooker that may or may not have been a guy in drag. Townes had just about given up, figuring the entire vendetta to be pointless, when he tailed Koblanski for what would he vowed would be the last time. That's when things got interesting. Up until that moment, Koblanski had conducted all of his illegal dealings in the open, seemingly without a care in the world. This clandestine meeting was different. Either Koblanski didn't want to be seen, or whomever he was meeting wanted to remain hidden from public scrutiny. If only Townes knew what the other cop was doing inside a condemned building illegally sapping power from the city.

Harry Townes barely had time to register the sudden movement from behind his car. The quick, momentary fluctuation in light warned of someone moving—an almost imperceptible eclipse of a body passing in front of the outside source of light. It was the only warning Townes had before the back window of his car exploded.

The first shot missed Townes. The second shot tore into his arm as he turned the key in the ignition, the engine roaring to life. He ducked down in the seat, shifted into drive, and burned rubber as three more slugs slammed into his car from somewhere behind him. He glanced into his rearview mirror, catching just the glimpse of his shooter—not enough to recognize him, but enough to recognize the uniform of a New York City police officer.

"Fuck," growled Townes. It was a multi-purpose

curse, expressing the pain of being shot, the fear racing through his brain, and the condemnation of his own arrogance. He'd underestimated Koblanski. The old cop must've had someone watching his back—maybe the entire time Townes had been tailing him. All that illegal activity for three days straight, carried out in the open, and not once did Townes consider that Koblanski might have someone watching his back. That person would've told Koblanski that Townes was on to him. And Koblanski would've told that person to wait. Wait until they were in the right part of town, where they could hit Townes, and no one would know what happened. Fuck. How could he be so stupid?

Townes realized that he was more than screwed. He was fucked. Koblanski had his minions throughout the department, and Townes knew, as the bullet wound in his arm screamed at him, that he'd been made, set-up, and targeted. He never figured Koblanski or any of his corrupt cohorts would ever resort to killing another cop, and it almost cost him his life. Now that they'd made their move, he was as good as dead.

Agonizing pain radiated throughout Townes's arm like an electric current. He had to get to an emergency room. The problem, of course, was going to be how to explain his gunshot wound. And even then, that wasn't the real problem. The real problem was that another cop had just tried to kill him, which meant he'd been targeted. There was no place safe for him to go. He wasn't screwed. He was fucked.

Tears of pain, frustration, and fear pooled in his eyes as he sped down the street, looking for any sign of pursuit. Any second now, a patrol car, or an unmarked vehicle was going to close in on him, and tear him to shreds. They'd come up with an explanation later. They'd frame him as being corrupt, or frame someone else. All of this would happen, provided he didn't bleed to death first.

He pulled his car over at the first subway stop he saw. Townes had to get out of his car—it made too easy of a target, with its shattered rear window. He glanced around in all directions—no sign of pursuing vehicles, but he was pretty sure he could hear sirens. Hell, he knew he heard sirens. It was, after all, Harlem, and the sirens of the police were the closest things to a philharmonic orchestra this far north.

Townes dragged himself out of his car with more grace than most people with a hole from a .38 police service revolver could muster. His adrenaline pumped, keeping his mind focused, and reigning in the pain as he made his way to the subway. He thought of hot-wiring a car—a trick he'd learned during his youth—but there was no time. His skills were rusty, and the chances of Koblanski's hit squad finding him, head under a steering wheel, fumbling with wires as he tried to start a car was simply too great. The subway provided a bullshit option, but the only one that made sense as the seconds ticked by.

"Think, you stupid son of a bitch," Townes mumbled to himself. He had to figure out where to go. Where to hide. He needed get the bullet removed, and he needed to get patched up, and he needed to live long enough to make sure he killed Koblanski. The only problem was that he didn't know how to do any of these things before shock set in, and he bled to death.

Standing alone on the subway platform, fashioning a miserable excuse for a tourniquet with his belt, Townes fought the urge to admit he had lost. He just needed a sign—something to help him know what to do next. A downtown express train pulled to a stop at the station, and in an instant, Townes knew what to do. At this time of night, the express train would get him to Times Square in a matter of minutes. If he was lucky, he might find someone there that could help him. Someone that could keep him alive.

"John Shaft," Townes said to himself. "He knows how to stitch a wound."

# NINETEEN

Shaft stared at the box sitting on the other side of his desk for hours. Abraham Scher had taken his leave, and Shaft sat, contemplating the philosophical nature behind what the box was said to contain. As much as he hated to play the role of philosopher, Shaft felt that the truth wasn't something that could be contained in a box. And if in fact there was some sort of truth that could be placed into a box, Shaft wasn't sure that he wanted to know about it.

Not to give it too much thought—lest he run the risk of engaging in the pointless task of philosophizing—but it seemed to Shaft that the truth was pretty much like the air. He stopped himself at that thought. Trying to explain to himself how the truth was like the air would make him crazier than thinking about the nameless broads he'd balled, the Viet Cong he'd killed, or the overall meaning of life, which on most days seemed to have little meaning. So, instead, he stared at the box, feeling a sense of dread at what truth might be hiding inside.

Hours passed, with Shaft doing nothing but staring at the box, and trying really hard not to think about the nature of what was and was not true. Every now and then he thought about having a drink, but the voice in his head—the one that usually encouraged him to pick up the bottle, or seek diversion of a more carnal nature—seemed to have a grim resolve. This sense of intense determination came from a dark place inside of Shaft's soul, where memories of his youth were kept contained in a box that he tried to keep under lock and key.

*See*, he thought to himself, *you can keep the truth in a box.*

Watching Cookie Venable die had knocked the lock off the box inside of Shaft. Seeing the young shooter, getting shot himself, all helped to open the box he kept inside himself, and managed to ignore with the help of booze and broads. But now there was a very real box in front of him, and it only served to remind him of the box he carried around inside his very being.

At some point, Shaft got up, walked to the other side of his desk, and sat in the chair that had been previously occupied by Abraham Scher. Shaft never sat in that chair. He never saw his office from that particular point of view—never saw his world from the same perspective as all those who had sat in the same chair. He was pretty sure that at some point Knocks Persons had sat in that chair. Or had he? Did Knocks ever come to the office?

Suddenly, Shaft couldn't remember if Knocks Persons had ever been in his office, and he realized the fragile nature of the truth, dependent upon something as unreliable as memory. He could, if he chose to do so, say that Knocks had been in his office, had sat in that particular chair, and in time, it would become his truth, even if it wasn't a definite truth.

*Fuck you, Johnny*, he said to himself. *Stop thinking so damn much.*

He opened the box, using an old switchblade knife to cut the tape. "What the fuck is this?" Shaft asked aloud.

The first thing Shaft saw—the thing sitting on the very top of the box—was a plain, sealed envelope, with his name and office address written on the front. Immediately under the envelope was a stack of cash. Under the cash there was more stuff—papers and photos and random artifacts of someone else's life. It became clear to Shaft that the box had been packed in a very specific manner. At least that's what his instincts told him, which meant he needed to go through the box in the order in which it had been meant for him to go through.

Shaft opened the envelope. Inside he found a hand-written letter, dated just over a week prior. The penmanship of the letter was impeccable—clean, crisp, and easy to read. The paper upon which the letter had been written had no lines, yet the writing itself lay on the sheet with a precise uniformity, each letter lining up perfectly to the next, forming words that lined up with equal perfection, creating something that almost resembled a work of art.

The letter started out simply enough, with his name.

John Shaft,

I am dead. There is no other way you would be reading this letter, other than the unavoidable truth that I have met my demise, which I suspect will be any day now. The fact that I have lived this long strikes me as a miracle, for I have done enough to earn my death many times over. I confess to you, out of respect, that the only regret surrounding my all too inevitable murder is that it comes at a time when, more than any other time, I have important things to do.

I have made my life as a criminal. You know this. I say it with no shame, and no pride, merely a matter of fact. To feel pride or shame at this juncture of my life would be pointless. It is important, however, that you understand this about my life: I see it for what it is, what it was, and the legacy I leave behind. I see it not through the eyes that I once saw things, but through the eyes of a father whose daughter was sadly damaged by a world I helped create. Seeing the world through this perspective has changed me. It is this change that has led to my murder.

By now, you may have heard that I was trying to stop the flow of drugs through Harlem. I knew I could not stop it altogether, but I had hoped that I could keep it from becoming worse than it already is. The thought of better people than me, losing their children the way I almost lost my daughter, has become a weight too heavy for me to carry, and it drove me to try and do something to change the world I helped create. It was a foolish attempt on my part, and not one that I can explain, other than to say I hope you never come to a point in your life where you realize everything you did, you could have done differently. As the time of my death grows closer, this is the realization I will take to my grave.

I do not know who will kill me, not specifically. But I know that the police will not investigate my murder in such a manner as to bring the killers to justice. The police, in fact, will no doubt be involved in my death. They have never wanted drugs out of Harlem, or crime, or any of the ills that have plagued the place I call home. Trust me, I know this to be a fact, just as I know my death within the next few days is a given.

The reason I turn to you, John Shaft, of all the people I know, is because you are the only person I have ever met with sense of justice. I do not want revenge. There are several people I could pay to find my killers, and do to them what they have done to me. You are not one of those people. You are many things, but you are not a killer for hire. You will, however, work to find who did this, and make sure that they pay in a manner that you think is appropriate, because you see a bigger picture than most. So many of us do not see the bigger picture, or, like myself, they do not see until it is too late.

I have taken the liberty to pay you for your services. If you chose not to take the case, I understand. Whoever kills me, will be dangerous. You know this as well as I do, and I will respect your decision to not put your life in danger, if that is what you decide. I have, however, left you certain items that may help in your investigation, if you chose to pursue this matter. These items represent who I was, and the world I came from. It is, I am reminded, a world you came from as well. We are more alike than either of us will ever care to admit, and our lives are bound in ways that you specifically

do not know, but deserve to understand. If there has ever been any
aspect of my life where I could consider myself a coward, it is in keeping certain truths from you. This box
contains truths you need to know,
and for better or worse, I suppose,
will determine how you proceed
from this point forward.

Thank you for your time and
consideration.
Norville "Knocks" Persons

Shaft read the letter a second time, then a third,
convinced it must have been some kind of practical
joke. No way had Knocks Persons just hired Shaft
from beyond the grave to solve his murder. Of all the
ridiculous things Shaft could think of, this topped the
list. The letter didn't even sound like Knocks, a man
of fewer words than Shaft himself. Knocks was gruff,
and mean, and ruthless. Knocks did not possess the
eloquence revealed in the letter Shaft read three times.

And yet, Knocks Persons was also the same man
who spoke in broken German, as he carried Abraham
Scher from the impending death of a concentration
camp. Knocks Person was the man who cried in front
of Shaft over the horrific things his daughter had done

and endured.

Hell, Shaft didn't know the first thing about Knocks Persons—at least not like he thought he did. He didn't know about Persons serving in World War II, or his involvement with that cop, Harry Townes. Up until the man had hired him, Shaft didn't even know Knocks had a daughter. Shaft had no clue what Knocks's handwriting looked like, or if that big, ugly son of a bitch, who talked mostly in gravely grunts, was the most eloquent motherfucker when it came to expressing himself via the written word.

Shaft thought of Etheridge Knight, the poet who wrote from prison while doing an eight-year bid for robbery. Areltha Havens had a copy of Knight's book, *Poems from Prison*, sitting on her bookshelf. Shaft hadn't picked it up and read it until after Arletha had been murdered. He read every book she had, trying to find a connection with a woman who'd become a ghost. Not much for poetry, something about Knight's poems resonated with Shaft. In particular, the poem "Feeling Fucked Up," reminded him of Arletha.

The first time Shaft read "Feeling Fucked Up," he cried. He stopped reading it after a point, but only because he'd memorized every word, line, and stanza. Etheridge Knight was a criminal and a poet, the same way Malcolm X had been a genius, trapped for a time in the body of a dope-dealing pimp. Shaft had known plenty of people who were so much more than their circumstances dictated. Wonder Wanda, to whom he lost his virginity in exchange for some shoplifted groceries, could sing like an angel. And she would draw the most beautiful pictures of landscapes that she'd never even come close to seeing from the view of her bedroom window in the projects.

In a moment of deep shame, John Shaft hated himself for doubting that Knocks Persons had written the letter. He hated himself for being audacious enough to think he knew enough about a man who existed as a living legend, when in fact, all he knew was the legend, and little more.

The only thing Shaft really knew for sure about Knocks Persons was what he knew about most people, himself included: most people were more complicated than they appeared. That was the most truthful truth, Shaft knew, and this particular truth was always kept inside the box each person carried around inside of them. Bits and pieces of the unrestrained honesty of who you are at the very core of your being slipped out from time to time. It could be found in the conversations you had with yourself, or in the poems you wrote while locked in a prison cell, or the way you sang a song from within the concrete walls of a tenement project, or the way you wrote a letter when you knew you were about to die. It reared up at a time when both the truth and the lies became too much, and all you could do was pick up the phone at half-past-too-late-to-call anyone, like Knocks Persons had done the night he was killed, and simply say, "I need your help."

With his death being the most immediate truth Knocks Persons could ever face, he called John Shaft and asked for help. Facing the same truth, he had written a letter that revealed more about him than Shaft had ever known. Knocks Persons knew he was going to die, and he had taken the time to write a letter to Shaft, and pack up a box full of…what? Clues? Truth? He had done all of this before he called and asked for help. It had been on his mind at least a day before the call.

Shaft held the letter in his hand, afraid to see what other truth could be hiding in this box—the Truth According to Knocks Persons. It began to sink in, the reality of it all, the total, and unrelenting honesty of the situation, which left him both perplexed and, in a way he couldn't really articulate, completely pissed off. Shaft felt a flood of emotions that he couldn't fully explain, even though he knew the source. It was the fact that when the shit was about to hit the fan, and Knocks Persons was about to die, the only person he felt comfortable to reach out to was Shaft.

*What the hell am I supposed to do?* Shaft asked himself.

Before he could start to think of an answer, the phone on Shaft's desk rang. He looked at his watch, and realized it was close to the same time that Knocks Persons had called him a week prior—it was nearly half-past-too-late-to-call. Shaft hated late, unexpected calls, especially when they came from people facing death. He thought for at least four rings that if it were a matter of life and death, the other person needed to make peace with their creator. Then he answered the phone.

"This is John Shaft."

The voice on the other end was faint, barely audible. "It's Harry Townes. I've been shot. I need your help."

"This is all a bunch of bullshit," Shaft mumbled, as he grabbed his gun, made sure it was loaded, put on his coat, and headed out the door.

# TWENTY

Shaft had seen men in far worse shape than police detective Harry Townes. He himself had been in far worse shape more times than he cared to remember. The big difference had been the conditions surrounding those particular instances. Even when he'd been shot up in the jungles of Vietnam, it was still a favorable set of circumstances to what he now faced in his tiny office overlooking Times Square.

Shaft had hurried down to the phone booth across the street from the Port Authority bus terminal, where he found Townes, looking like shit. Shaft helped the cop back to his office, the two men looking like a couple of drunks stumbling their way down the street in a haze of booze-soaked uncertainty. Townes, weak, slipping deeper and deeper into shock, explained everything in faint whispers, causing Shaft to look over his shoulder every few steps. He'd rushed out of his office to help a walking dead man, and in doing so had potentially placed a target on his own back.

The tourniquet Townes had fashioned from his belt had stopped the bleeding, but the bleeding was just icing on a cake of shit. No exit wound meant the bullet had taken up residence in the police detective's arm. And the fact that there was no telling how many corrupt cops were out hunting Townes meant that the entire city of New York was a place where danger walked a beat, and patrolled the streets in cars with sirens and flashing lights. To be the prey of predators like the New York Police Department meant you were looking at being fucked in every orifice of your body, only it wouldn't be cocks violating you, it would be bullets.

Shaft helped Townes ease into the chair he'd sat in while reading the letter from Knocks Persons. Shaft kicked the box out of the way, as he laid pages of the *New York Times* on the floor. Something would need to absorb the blood, and Shaft had no towels or sheets in his office, and the box of tissues wouldn't do the trick.

John Shaft moved with a speed and efficiency that betrayed him as a man of action, capable of operating with an instinct few people ever possessed. That instinct extended far beyond self-preservation, or his ability to kill—it reached out into an area of danger, where death lurked, and only a rare breed of person possessed the skills to grapple with the Grim Reaper over one of its intended victims.

To be sure, death had a grip on Harry Townes, though the firmness of the grip had yet to be determined. Shaft picked up the switchblade knife sitting on top of his desk, leaned over the top, and reached into the bottom drawer, where he pulled out his bottle of Johnnie Walker, a book of matches, and his first aid kit.

"Where's your wallet?" Shaft asked.

"J…jacket pocket," said Townes.

Shafted reached into Townes's jacket pocket, pulled out his wallet—a small, well-worn piece of black leather. He handed the wallet to Townes. "Here. Hold this," said Shaft. Townes weakly held on to the wallet.

Shaft flicked open the knife, lit several matches, and held the flame to the blade until the matches had burned down so low the fire singed his fingertips and the heat had sterilized the metal.

"Put the wallet in your mouth, and bite down on it," Shaft said.

Townes placed the wallet in his mouth just as Shaft poured whiskey on to the bullet wound. The scream of pain was more of a muffled roar, absorbed by the wallet.

"This is going to hurt like a motherfucker," Shaft

said. "Here goes."

Shaft gripped around the entry wound with his left hand, as he used his right hand to probe the wound with the blade of the knife.

Townes lurched in pain, biting down on his wallet so hard he felt he'd tear a chunk out of it.

"Hold the fuck still," growled Shaft. "Moving makes it harder. Harder makes it take longer. Taking longer makes it hurt more."

It took Shaft a full minute, if not slightly longer, to find the bullet. He managed to pull it out; both his hand and the .38 slug were covered in blood, though the bullet appeared intact. Not that it mattered; he'd done all he could do under the circumstances. If there were any fragments of the slug left in Townes, there was a better chance he'd die from at least three other things than a little bit of a bullet. And those three things didn't include the cops out looking for him.

Shaft dropped the bullet onto the newspaper on the floor, which had caught the blood flowing from the wound. Fortunately, the tourniquet had slowed the blood flow. Otherwise, Shaft was convinced, Townes would've bled out by now.

Townes's breathing labored as his consciousness slowly slipped away. Shaft poured more Johnnie Walker over the wound, which had the effect of a charge of electricity shooting through Townes.

"Calm the fuck down," said Shaft. "Pain means you're still alive."

Shaft didn't bother to wipe the blood off his hands before he started to stitch up the wound. By the time the second suture was done, Townes had passed out from the pain. Shaft laughed to himself, wanted to call Townes a pussy, but he knew that wasn't the case.

With Townes unconscious, it made Shaft's work easier. He stitched up the wound, walked down hall to the restroom he shared with other tenants on the third floor, and washed his hands. Shaft returned to his office, made sure that Townes hadn't died during his absence, and then took a bandage from his first aid kit and applied it to the police detective's wound.

Shaft knew that Townes needed real medical attention, and real protection, neither of which seemed like real possibilities in New York. There were very few things John Shaft couldn't get within the city of New York, but outside of the five boroughs was a different story altogether. Any chance of keeping Townes alive, and safe, would be somewhere beyond the city limits.

It was too late to call anyone, but calls needed to be made anyway. He needed to figure out how to get Townes out of the city, and he needed to figure out where to hide the wounded detective. Neither would be easy. For all Shaft knew, every fucking flat-foot pig in the city was looking for Townes.

Shaft picked up the phone and made the first of what would be no more than two phone calls. If he ever had to make more than two calls for anything, he knew he wasn't trying hard enough—hadn't called the right people. As the phone rang, he looked over at Townes, and then the box sitting just a few feet away. If there was either a Heaven or a Hell, Knocks Persons must've been watching Shaft with a twisted sense of enjoyment.

Someone answered the phone, his voice tired and pissed at the fact that anyone would be calling at this hour. "This better be fucking good," said Vic Anderozzi.

"Vic. It's John Shaft. I'm drowning in shit, and it ain't even my own shit."

# TWENTY-ONE

Shaft took a calculated risk dragging Vic Anderozzi into the shit storm that rapidly seemed to be escalating into a hurricane. Shaft could count on one hand the people he truly trusted, and that included those that were still alive. When it came to the police, Shaft didn't trust them at all. Anderozzi was the closest thing to an exception to that rule, insomuch that Shaft trusted him as much as he could trust any cop. He and Anderozzi had a game they played with each other, at least that's how Shaft thought of it. He called the game Need-to-Know, meaning he and Anderozzi never lied to each other, nor were they ever completely forthcoming with the truth. Instead, they told each other what each of them deemed the other needed to know. It was as close to a trusting relationship Shaft could ever have with a cop, or just about any other living human being.

Need-to Know was a game that had no official

rulebook, and could only be played on instinct. The better your instinct, the better you were at the game. Unlike other games, the point of Need-to-Know was to have both players win. Shaft had played Need-to-Know with Anderozzi several times, and the fact that neither had died, and that Shaft hadn't gone to prison, meant both were winners. Hell, one of the times they'd played the game, Anderozzi ended being awarded a commendation. Anderozzi had even confessed that the night after the award ceremony, his wife gave him some ass for the first time in nearly six months. That was an example of Need-to-Know not being needed, though it summed up how far both men could extend the rules of play.

By calling Anderozzi, Shaft had put his ass on the line more than he'd just done by digging a bullet out of Townes and stitching him back together. As it was, Shaft was caught in a game of Need-to Know with Townes, who he didn't really know, which made the game difficult as hell. Playing the game with more than one cop at a time was like dancing with multiple partners. Three people couldn't dance a waltz together. The best they could do was form a kick line. Shaft wasn't sure he was prepared to link arms with Townes and Anderozzi and perform with the choreographed precision of the Rockettes.

More important than that, Shaft didn't know how

Anderozzi would respond to the current state of affairs. Shaft believed in his heart and soul that if there were ever a cop that could not be corrupted—who actually believed in justice—it had to be Vic Anderozzi. At the same time, no one was beyond corruption. Everyone had a price for which they would sell their soul. Some people knew their asking price, and others, like himself and Anderozzi, simply had never been made an offer that seemed worth the price. Though if he were to be totally honest with himself—which he wasn't prepared to do at the moment—Shaft suspected he had actually sold his soul years ago, back in 1962. He'd been seventeen, facing a conviction as an adult, and the judge gave him a choice of prison, or joining the military. Shaft chose to not go to prison, a decision that led to joining the Marines, ending up in Vietnam by '65, and taking more lives than he cared to remember, but could never forget.

If John Shaft had been completely corrupted—if he had in fact sold his soul—the deal had been made that day in 1962 in the courtroom. The transaction was made complete a few years later with his first confirmed kill in the Mekong Delta, three months, two weeks, and a few hours before his twentieth birthday.

Shaft had no delusions about being a good man. He wasn't evil like the men that had imprisoned Abraham Scher, and butchered more than six million Jews.

At the same time, in the deal that quite probably cost him his soul, Shaft had become one of those men that followed orders, and in doing so, there were more than two dozen lives he could lay claim to having taken. Shaft wondered how many deaths could be hung on your name—whether it was as a soldier, or a cop, or a dope pusher, or merely an apathetic motherfucker who did nothing for anyone, while the world starved to death—before you could be considered evil. Was there some sort of mathematic equation? How far was he from crossing the line, or was he already an evil man?

Townes continued to breathe, and though Shaft checked the man's pulse, he didn't really know much about pulses, other than the fact that none at all was a bad thing. He knew he had time until Anderozzi showed up, either agreeing to help him, or telling him to go fuck himself. Shaft needed to start planning ahead—planning for when the storm got worse, with gale force winds, and torrential rain, and flooding, and the wrath of God, the likes of which had not been seen since Noah built the ark, and everyone around him thought he was a stupid motherfucker for doing so.

Rather than sit around and wait for Anderozzi to show up, Shaft took advantage of the time he had. He gathered up the box, carried it down the hall, and then down to the lobby of the building that housed his office. In the back of the lobby sat a door leading to a rear corridor that connected his building to one next door, and one on the other block. The corridor housed rear entrance doors to all three buildings, a maintenance closet full of cleaning supplies, and a storage closet for the adult bookstore that occupied the building opposite Shaft's office. The rear of the adult bookstore had a door that led to the back corridor, which made it Shaft's secret exit and entrance in and out of his office building.

He carried the box to the maintenance closet, unscrewed the grate covering a ventilation shaft, and hid the box inside. Shaft had no idea if anyone else knew about the box, or would come looking for it, but he had decided long ago that the difference between being paranoid and precautious wasn't determined until it was too late. The competition between the two always came down to a photo-finish at the end of the race or with the judges' decision at the end of the fifteenth round. If he kept score of such things, he'd have to say that he'd been precautious more often than he'd been paranoid, though in the moment it was always impossible to guess which would claim the victory.

By the time he got back to his office, Shaft felt certain that his actions had been more paranoia than precaution. He sat at his desk, lit a cigarette, and realized that he didn't want a drink. Not wanting a taste of

Johnnie Walker—the only man Shaft truly loved—felt strange. With all the thinking he'd been doing, Johnnie should've been his go-to guy. But for some reason, Shaft knew that the comfort he'd find in a bottle of whiskey would actually prove to be a distraction, and he didn't want any distractions right now. Feeling good didn't seem as important as having a clear head.

Shaft had checked Townes's pulse a dozen more times, wondered if maybe he should say a prayer—a thought that made him laugh out loud—and smoked two more cigarettes before Anderozzi arrived.

"Holy shit. Is that Harry Townes?" asked Anderozzi.

"You know him?" asked Shaft.

"Only by reputation, really. They call him Saint Harry."

"What do you call him?" Shaft asked.

"From what I know, I call him a good cop. A damn good cop," Anderozzi said.

"That's good enough for me," said Shaft. He went on to tell Anderozzi how he'd met Townes at the scene of Knocks Persons's murder.

"You were there?" asked Anderozzi. "You're name isn't in any of the reports."

Shaft looked at Anderozzi for a moment. In their game of Need-to-Know, Anderozzi had just filled Shaft in on a major need-to-know—that for whatever reason, the police lieutenant had read the reports on a case he wasn't working.

"Look, we can stand around here jawing, or we can do something to make sure this cat doesn't die," Shaft said. "There's people on the force that want him dead, which means we've got to get him out of the city, and stash him some place safe. Preferably some place where a real doctor can make sure my butcher job doesn't kill this poor motherfucker."

Shaft and Anderozzi carried Townes down to the street, laying him out in the back of Anderozzi's car. Both Shaft and Anderozzi looked around to see if anyone had witnessed them. More specifically, they looked to see if there were any cops in sight.

"Where are we taking him?" Shaft asked.

"I know a guy in Jersey," said Anderozzi. "Can't remember where we are currently, but I think he owes me a favor. If not, I'll owe him when this is done."

The engine of Anerozzi's car roared to life. "There wasn't anything on the police radio about Townes during the drive over here—that means whoever is behind this hit is trying to keep it off the radar."

"Is that good for us?" asked Shaft.

Anderozzi turned to look at Townes in the backseat. "No," said the police lieutenant. "Nothing is good for us right now."

There was a matter-of-factness in Anderozzi's

statement that made Shaft feel a twinge of guilt. Whatever was going on, it wasn't Vic's fight, until now.

Shaft pulled out two cigarettes, placed both in his mouth, and lit them. He handed one of them to Anderozzi, who mumbled a thanks.

"Vic, I'm sorry I dragged you into this. I didn't know what else to do."

Anderozzi took a drag off the cigarette, holding the smoke for a second or two longer than he normally would have done. He slowly exhaled. "No. It's okay. I'm glad you called," said Anderozzi.

"Really?" Shaft asked.

"Yeah. Because I know you'd do right by me if I was the one lying in the backseat."

Shaft stared intently out the passenger side window of Anderozzi's car, as the driver turned west on to 42$^{nd}$ Street, heading toward the Lincoln Tunnel.

"Okay," said Shaft. "Let me tell you what's going on." With that, Shaft told Anderozzi everything. He didn't hold back any of the facts, except where he'd hidden the box. But he told the cop about the letter, and the cash, and ghost of Knocks Persons essentially hiring Shaft from beyond the grave.

"I swear to God, Johnny, no one gets into as much trouble as you," said Anderozzi.

"C'mon, Vic, you know me. I don't get into any of this shit on purpose," Shaft said.

"No, not on purpose. You're just a goddamn shit magnet."

Shaft shrugged his shoulders. He couldn't argue with that assessment. He did, in fact, have a penchant for attracting shit.

# TWENTY-TWO

Shaft smoked a cigarette, watching the sunrise off in the distance, somewhere to the east, far beyond the island of Manhattan. From where he sat, he couldn't see a single trace of the city. For him, the moment the skyline of New York disappeared from view, it meant he'd ventured into another world. A mix of low-hanging clouds and unidentifiable pollution hung in the air, which Shaft added to with an exhale of cigarette smoke and a stream of profanity he mumbled under his breath.

He didn't know exactly where he was—somewhere west of Newark, in one of those small New Jersey towns with a weird name. Shaft looked around cautiously, like a predatory jungle cat in unfamiliar hunting grounds. Shaft only knew two places really well, New York City and the jungles of Vietnam. Everyplace else was just that—somewhere else. Even this place, less than an hour from the Big Apple, was somewhere else. To make matters worse, this somewhere else was located in Jersey, one of those places where Shaft had no one. He'd served with a few guys from Jersey, but that was his only connection to the Garden State.

Vic Anderozzi drove through the Lincoln Tunnel, took the 495 to the 95 to the 280, and then took an exit just before the Garden State Parkway, which placed them somewhere west of I-don't-know-where-the-fuck-I-am. The only things Shaft knew for sure was that he was somewhere uncomfortably white, and that he was deep in DeCavalcante territory. To the best of his knowledge, Shaft had never dealt with anyone from the New Jersey crime family—at least not directly. He knew that "Sam the Plumber" DeCavalcante still called the shots from his prison cell, but that was about it. He'd heard a wild rumor that for a while, the term "pulling a Shaft" had made the rounds in the Jersey underworld—a phrase that meant you'd killed somebody.

The story had come to him a few years earlier, after an encounter with Sal Venneri, a mob underboss in New York. No one could prove that Shaft had killed the gangster, but there were those who talked about it in hushed whispers. There had been no love between DeCavalcante and Venneri, and the rumor, as Shaft had heard it, was that the Jersey crime boss actually drank a toast to him, and for a time, any hit ordered by Sam the Plumber was made by him saying, "It's time to pull a Shaft."

Shaft never knew for sure if this was true or not—if he'd become some sort of urban legend amongst the Jersey goombas—and as he took a final drag of his cigarette, he thought about what it meant to have the act of killing bestowed with your name. The word murder had its origins in several old European languages, derived from words like the Old English "morthor" and the Dutch "moord"—something Shaft learned during his time as a student at NYU. But as far as he knew, none of those words came from a person's name. He doubted some Old English gangsters decided to coin a term after some cat named Morthor killed his neighbor over a dispute involving sheep grazing on his land.

Shaft and Anderozzi arrived at a large house that had been converted into some sort of doctor's office or medical clinic. They had made one stop along the way, just long enough for Anderozzi to make a call from a pay phone. Shaft assumed that the tired looking man that met them outside the clinic had been the recipient of Vic's phone call. The man looked not only tired, but pissed off—pissed off the way people look when they're asked for a favor that they have to repay, even when they don't want to.

Anderozzi and the tired, pissed off man shared a

few heated words in Italian. Shaft had never heard Vic speak in Italian before. A third man hovered off to the side of the two men arguing in Italian. Shaft recognized the man as muscle. Built like a boxer who had stopped boxing, the man had a crooked nose, probably broken in a fight, either in the ring, or after getting smashed in the face with the butt of a gun. The bulge on the inside of his jacket told Shaft that the man carried a big gun, and didn't give a shit who knew about it.

After a few minutes of arguing between Anderozzi and his irritated friend, Shaft and muscle man got the go-ahead to carry Harry Townes out of the car, and into the old house. Anderozzi and the other man led the way as Shaft and his helper carried Townes into the building. With the exception of their labored breathing and a few grunts of frustration, they struggled in silence, hauling the unconscious, dead weight of Townes down a flight of stairs and into the basement.

The basement looked like a hospital operating room. In fact, it was an operating room—something that looked like it didn't really belong in an otherwise average-looking doctor's office in a New Jersey suburb. Shaft had only seen the uptown versions of rooms like this one—rooms that were not this clean or well stocked—where men like Doc Powell made late-night calls to remove bullets or stitch up knife wounds.

*Fuck*, Shaft thought to himself. *Vic Anderozzi, the most honest cop I know, has taken me to a mob doctor.*

Shaft and the muscle man laid Townes down on an operating table. Tired man whispered something to Anderozzi, who looked over at Shaft. "Johnny, it's probably best if you wait outside," Anderozzi said.

Shaft stared at Anderozzi for a moment, not saying a word, but the cop gave him a knowing, slightly reassuring nod. Shaft knew that whatever was going to happen was going to happen, and he'd have to deal with it later. He'd put his trust in Anderozzi, like placing a bet on a roulette table, and now it was time to double down.

It only felt like an eternity while Shaft sat on a tiny bench outside the doctor's office, watching the sunrise, thinking about more things than he cared to think about even on his best days. He glanced down at his watch, and realized he'd only been outside for around thirty minutes. He'd have smoked another cigarette, but there were none left in the pack. He would've had a drink, but his bottle was back in his office. He'd have gotten laid, but he didn't know any chicks in Jersey, and it was too early to go out looking. So, instead he sat and thought and waited, and wondered what he had gotten himself into—a thought he had far too often.

In moments like these, Shaft regretted having dropped out of college and not gotten his law degree. Not that he'd ever had a moment like this outside of a mob doctor's office in Jersey—nor had he even imagined that he would. Still, it was the what-the-fuck-have-I-gotten-myself-into moments that caused Shaft to rethink his life decisions. He felt like he was having a mid-life crisis, which was impossible, because he wasn't even in his thirties yet. Of course, the way he'd lived thus far, maybe being in his late twenties was old age for him. Maybe the pressing weight he felt on his soul, and the thoughts that plagued his mind, were the result of someone who'd lived several lifetimes in just over twenty-five years.

"Johnny, why don't you come inside now," said Anderozzi.

Anderozzi had stepped outside, unnoticed by Shaft. The police detective's sleeves were rolled up, and he wore surgical gloves covered in blood.

Shaft stood up, and fought the urge to hug Anderozzi. Not because he was happy to see the cop, but simply because he was thankful that someone had come and rescued him from his own thoughts. As much as Shaft didn't care for the company of others, he really hated being alone with his own thoughts.

# TWENTY-THREE

Red Linny Morton weighed his options, but they kept coming up the same—he was going to have to take out a cop. He might even have to take out several cops, which didn't bother him from any sort of moral standpoint. The problem with killing cops was that it always involved a lot of work, especially after the fact, because those motherfuckers always took that kind of stuff personally. It was easy to pay the police off when it came to a murder investigation, but getting them to look the other way with one of their own was never easy.

Koblanski warned Red Linny that a detective had been snooping around on the Knocks Persons murder, but he said there wasn't a thing to worry about. "I got it covered," Koblanski said.

Only problem was that the dumb fuck didn't have it covered. The hit went sideways, and Detective Townes had gone missing. It wasn't Townes that had

Morton concerned—that was Koblanski's problem. No, Red Linny's concerns were about Koblanski himself. If that corrupt son of a bitch ever found himself in real trouble, he'd put on a dress, don blackface, and sing like Gladys Knight if it meant staying out of jail. Red Linny almost laughed at the thought of Koblanksi wearing a dress, face blacked by burnt cork, singing about leaving on a midnight train to Georgia. Perhaps Morton could convince the corrupt cop to put on a show for him, before having him whacked. Or better yet, Red Linny could kill Koblanski while the cop was in blackface and wearing a dress. That would make for one hell of a crime scene.

The fact that Koblanski had ordered a hit on Townes, and then blew it, meant that a door to trouble had been opened up. If Townes lived, he could point a finger at Koblanski. And if Townes died, there was always a chance that an investigation would lead back to Koblanski. If that were the case, Koblanski would start giving up names left and right, starting with the Puerto Ricans, then the blacks, and finally the Italians, in that order. In which case, he would have to be taken care of, which really meant that he needed to be eliminated before he had a chance to become a problem.

Having Koblanski killed wouldn't be easy. On top of that, Red Linny could think of at least three other cops that would need to be taken out in the process.

He'd have to reach out to his man in Florida to see if there were any crazy Haitians that could be sent in to do the job. That in and of itself was a dangerous proposition, and in a perfect world, the last resort.

Red Linny made a mental list of who needed to be killed in addition to Koblanski—a list he arranged in his mind both alphabetically and by order of importance. He often did things like that, as if it were some sort of game. He kept lists in his head of everyone he killed, each one filled with the same names, but arranged in different order. Morton had an alphabetical list, a chronological list, a list broken down by method of killing, and one by how much he enjoyed the act of killing.

Stan Koblanski's name was third on the alphabetical list of people that needed to be taken care of immediately, but first on the list of importance. The others on the list—all of them cops—would be difficult to deal with. Killing one cop would bring down a world of hurt, but getting rid of four or five—especially those cops in particular—would be a problem.

That's when the idea came to Red Linny—the idea of how to kill the cops, and who to get to do the job. The idea was pure genius, and it made his cock get hard just thinking about it. In his mind, where he made multiple lists of the same thing, only categorized differently, and where he fantasized about skull-fucking his victims, and where he meticulously planned and operated a crime organization that no one had the balls to fuck with, Red Linny had come up with the greatest idea of his life. The idea had nothing real to go with it, but those things came in time. All that mattered was that the man he hated most would do the killing and take the fall.

After all these years, Red Linny Morton would finally get even with John Shaft.

# TWENTY-FOUR

Shaft thought Harry Townes looked like day-old shit left out in the sun too long. At the same time, Shaft had seen guys look worse than Townes, and at least Townes was breathing. A bag of clear fluid hung from the I.V. stand next to the operating table. The tube running from the bag into Townes's arm steadily dripped the clear fluid that Shaft figured contained a feel-good mixture of painkillers and antibiotics.

The irritated-looking man stood at a sink, scrubbing his hands clean. He looked over at Shaft as the black detective entered the room with Anderozzi. With a nod of his head, while drying his hands, the man indicated Townes. "Good work," he said. "I opened him back up to make sure there were no bullet fragments, but you got the whole thing. Did a better than average job sewing him together, too."

"Thanks," said Shaft. No one had ever complimented him on his first aid skills before.

"You a medic?"

"No," said Shaft. "I'm a survivor."

The man extended his hand. "Steve. Dr. Steve Lucente."

"John Shaft." Shaft took the man's hand, looking him over for the first time. Dr. Lucente was a young man—Shaft guessed no more than thirty-five—and prettier than he was handsome. At first glance, Shaft thought of actor Sal Mineo, but that wasn't who the doctor truly resembled. Something about Lucente looked familiar, though Shaft couldn't place it.

"Uncle Vic tells me you served with Mario," Lucente said.

In an instant, Shaft realized why Dr. Steve Lucente looked so familiar. The man looked like a slightly older version of Corporal Mario Anderozzi, nephew of Vic Anderozzi, who had served with Shaft in Vietnam. Shaft liked Mario. He'd been there when the poor kid stepped on a landmine. Years later, when Shaft was just starting out as a private dick, he met Mario's Uncle Vic. Shaft seldom questioned such things, but at least once or twice he couldn't help but wonder if Mario had been pulling some strings from the land of the dead, bringing his uncle and his war buddy together.

"Mario was a good kid," said Shaft, walking over to examine Townes. He had no idea what to check for, but he hoped that his show of concern might keep the conversation from going back to Vietnam. No one needed the conversation going there.

"He'll be out of it for a while but he'll pull through," said Lucente. "I've seen worse."

"So have I," said Shaft. His eyes moved fastidiously, from Townes, to Lucente, to Anderozzi, to the muscle man hanging out in the corner, the gun no longer bulging out from under his coat, because his coat had been taken off and draped along the back of a chair.

Silence hung in the air, made heavy by unspoken truths. Shaft realized that not only had he walked into a world that Vic Anderozzi kept secret, he was now standing in the middle of this world of unrevealed truths, where matters of life and death were traded back and forth under the guise of favors. He couldn't help but wonder what price he'd have to pay for being admitted into this world. What price would Townes have to pay?

"This is family stuff, John," said Anderozzi. "Stuff I don't talk about too often."

"I figured that out already," Shaft said. "I'm sure if I had family, I'd have stuff like this too. Someday, when we got less to deal with, you can explain it all to me. Or not. It's up to you."

Anderozzi nodded without saying a word. Many of the conversations he and Shaft had consisted of nods, shrugs, and various hand gestures that took the place of verbal communication. It was a language they'd come to understand, along with their game of Need-to-Know.

"What about Townes?" asked Shaft.

Anderozzi walked over to Shaft's side, looking down at Townes on the operating table. "We wait here until he's up and aware, so that he knows he's safe," said Anderozzi. "Wouldn't want him waking up to the site of these ugly guineas—that'd be enough to scare the shit out of anyone."

"Then what?" asked Shaft.

"Then Steve and Vito take him someplace safe, while we do what we need to do."

Shaft looked over at the big muscle man. "You Vito?" Shaft asked.

Vito nodded his head.

"You always this talkative?" Shaft asked, not sure what to make of the big man.

Vito nodded again, this time adding in a hand gesture that seemed to indicate everything that was unfolding in the moment. "All this here," he said, "this is family. Uncle Vic knows you, you knew Mario, and that's enough for me. This is all free—no strings attached to you or Sleeping Beauty. We're doing this for Mario."

Shaft looked at the muscle man with a newfound perspective. He was more than the hired muscle he appeared to be, he was some kind of shot-caller.

"Understood," said Shaft. "You an Anderozzi or a Lucente?"

"Rutigliano," said Vito. "But we're all family."

"Well, if we're all family, I could go for some breakfast and some smokes," said Shaft.

# TWENTY-FIVE

Shaft thought for a man who'd been shot, twice operated on and sewn back together, and pumped full of who-knew-what painkillers and antibiotics, Harry Townes seemed to be talking too much. His words were slurred and slow, like a drunken man so liquored up his sweat smelled like booze, but they came at a steady pace that had become almost unrelenting. Shaft wondered how much of Townes's monologue came from the dope Dr. Lucente had fed into the I.V., and how much of it was the sum total of keeping shit pent up for too long.

His stomach full, Shaft sat with his eyes closed, his head resting against the passenger side window of Vic Anderozzi's car, as they retraced their route back to New York City. The original plan—if there every truly had been a plan—hadn't included returning to the city with Townes. Although it had never been directly discussed, Shaft had assumed they would stash Townes some place safe, though he had no idea where that might be, how long the wounded officer would stay hidden in this unknown location, or who would take care of him. All of that was what could be categorized in the "minor details" part of a master plan that may or may not have ever existed. None of Shaft's vague idea of a quasi-plan mattered, however, because it had become clear, shortly after Townes regained consciousness, that he had plans of his own.

There had been very little by way of arguing. Dr. Lucente told Townes, "I'd advise you to rest for the next few days." To which Townes responded by asking how long he'd been unconscious.

Shaft checked his watch. "You've been out of it close to twelve hours," he said, realizing that half a day had passed since Townes called him from the phone booth across from the Port Authority bus terminal.

"That's enough rest," Townes slurred.

Shaft, Anderozzi, Lucente, and Rutigliano all exchanged glances with each other, none of them saying a word. Each man searched within himself to find an argument against Townes, while simultaneously placing themselves in his position. Shaft couldn't speak for any of the others, but he knew that if it were him, he'd be reacting the same as Townes. Hell, he had been in the same spot before—backed into a corner, threatened, and certain his death was waiting at the end of the block, just around the corner. He'd felt this way more than once, going back more than half his life, and not once did he ever take the time to lie down and rest. He balled up his fists and came out swinging, or locked and loaded and came out shooting, or picked up the biggest stick or the nearest brick, and made sure that he did as much damage before his number was called.

Other men might have argued with Townes. Men with lesser convictions, who had never made a real decision about who lived and who died—who had never stood for anything on either side of the law—would have argued with Townes. But Townes was in a room with Vic Anderozzi, another cop with a clearly set moral compass, Vito Rutigliano and Steve Lucente, a gangster and a mob doctor related to Anderozzi by blood, and John Shaft. Townes couldn't have asked for a better, more eclectic simpatico group playing by their own rulebooks.

Shaft and Vito Rutigliano helped Townes into the backseat of Anderozzi's car. Dr. Lucente gave Townes a bottle of pills with the instructions of taking no more than one every six hours for pain. Anderozzi and his nephews exchanged a few words in Italian, and even though he didn't understand what was being said, Shaft had the uncomfortable feeling of someone who knows a secret they're not supposed to know.

Shaft and Anderozzi were more than acquaintances, but not really friends. Their relationship existed in an ambiguous state dictated by the immediate needs of the moment. Shaft knew that Anderozzi had a wife and kids, but he'd never met them, nor did he ever expect to meet them, because the nature of their relationship didn't dictate such familiarity. They shared drinks, and laughs, and told little stories of their lives that were neither too personal nor too revealing. And to be sure, they shared a few secrets, but nothing like the secret come to light over the last several hours.

Shaft understood that every man has the armor he wears in the outside world. That armor is forged through a lifetime of experiences—both good and bad—and it is what protects them from the constant siege of life. Within that armor is the true self, the secrets and the fears and the loves and the weaknesses that the armor is built to protect in the first place. Shaft realized that the armor was no different than the box each person used to hold his or her truths. He thought of the box Abraham Scher had delivered to his office.

Thinking about the box, Shaft's mind began turning. Everything led back to Knocks Persons. Townes had been shot because of Knocks Persons. Hell, Shaft himself had been grazed by a bullet because of Persons. He'd watched his childhood friend die on the front stoop of Persons's house. And now, he had been given a glimpse into the secret life of Vic Anderozzi, all courtesy of a gangster who'd been murdered only a week or so earlier.

Anderozzi gripped the steering wheel, as he slowly maneuvered through the beginning of rush hour traffic. Traffic heading west out of the city was gridlocked, and it wasn't much better heading into the city either. If the traffic bothered Anderozzi, he didn't let it show. While others leaned on their car horns, he simply took what came his way.

From the backseat, Townes continued to talk, though in reality he was mostly rambling—talking to himself in a drug-induced conversation that came out as an annoying hum.

Shaft felt like his sanity was slipping. He opened his eyes to the sight of an endless row of taillights before him, all leading a path back to some place very dangerous. The red lights struck Shaft as being some kind of warning, like it was time to stop, turn around, and get as much distance between him and Manhattan as possible. Or perhaps the red lights were the blinking eyes of demons, the blasts of car horns their shrieks, heading back into hell, and he and Anderozzi and Townes were blindly following these monsters toward damnation.

"Vic, I'm sorry I dragged you into this," Shaft said.

His sincerity was palpable, clinging to his words as they left his mouth, and filling the car with a feeling Shaft couldn't quite identify.

"If it was me that had come to you in the same position, what would you've done?" asked Anderozzi.

"Now that I know about your nephew the mob surgeon, I'd call him."

"Before you knew about him," said Anderozzi.

"I don't know. I would've thought of someone to call—found someone to help. I'd've dug the bullet out of you and stitched you up same as Townes back there," said Shaft.

"Then don't be sorry you dragged me into this."

"The fuck're you guysssssh talkin' 'bout?" slurred Townes.

"Shaft is telling me how much he loves me," said Anderozzi.

"Yeah, and you keep interrupting," said Shaft. "Go back to sleep so I can finish wooing this motherfucker."

"You two make a cute couple," Townes chuckled, followed by a groan of pain.

"Cute? There's nothing cute about us," said Shaft. "We're handsome, rugged, manly men—ain't a fuckin' thing cute about us."

"I don't know," said Anderozzi, "You do have cute eyes, Johnny. And I've always had a thing for that scar on your forehead."

"My scar isn't cute. My scar is rugged, yes. Manly, yes. Maybe even sexy…"

"Definitely sssssexy," slurred Townes, interrupting Shaft.

"Thank you," said Shaft. "Rugged, manly, and sexy. All that works for me. But my scar sure as fuck is not cute. None of my scars are cute."

"Fuck you," said Anderozzi. "I think it's cute."

"No, fuck you," Shaft said. "Now, if you wanna talk cute, we'll talk about that bald head of yours, Vic. I bet it drives all the girls crazy, the way it always shines just so when the light hits it the right way. Makes me swoon."

Laughter erupted in the car as traffic moved slowly closer to the city. The laughter cut through what was now steadily creeping towards being a full day of tension, pain, and uncertainty. For a moment, laughter was all that existed—mocking the cruel absurdity of life and death. No danger existed. There was no need to glance over your shoulder, to make sure the safety was off and a round was in the chamber. If the taillights before them were in fact the blinking eyes of demons leading the way back into hell, then laughter was their prayer of protection. It soothed them, and made them not worry that between the three of them they didn't have a clue, a plan, or a real prayer.

John Shaft, Vic Anderozzi, and Harry Townes laughed like nothing mattered. They laughed like they felt no pain, no fear, no regret, or any of those other emotions that men often clutched at when they needed their hands free for the fight that lay ahead. Chances were good—really good—that any or all of them would be dead in the very near future. They all knew this; just as surely as they knew that the sun was setting behind them in the west. And still, all they could do was laugh.

# TWENTY-SIX

Stan Koblanski couldn't shake the feeling that he might be in over his head. There had been other times in the past, when there had been a lot to handle, or things felt out of balance, but this felt different. This wasn't "things about to get out of control"—things were out of control. The ship had struck the iceberg and started sinking.

Koblanski didn't know how long Harry Townes had been keeping an eye on him, just that at some point the damn spade had become an unwanted shadow. He figured it had something to do with Knocks Persons's murder, though he couldn't figure out the angle. Townes's reputation for being an honest cop was the stuff of legend, but maybe it was all bull-shit. Maybe he'd been on Persons's payroll, and now he was looking to settle the score with whoever pulled the trigger on his boss. Koblanski could understand that.

What had him worried, however, was the possibility that Townes wasn't on the take, and instead was doing real cop work. This scared Koblanski almost as much as the psychotic behavior of Red Linny Morton. If Townes really was doing real police work, there was the danger he'd dig up some real shit—shit that went way beyond the killing of Knocks Persons.

It didn't really matter what was behind Townes's actions. All that mattered to Koblanski was dealing with the other cop before Townes became a real problem, and so he ordered a hit. It should've been simple. It should've looked like a cop being in the wrong place at the wrong time, being taken out by some anonymous street thug in Harlem. Instead, it had all turned into a giant clusterfuck.

Unless Townes had the courtesy to crawl off and die in some corner, where his body was yet to be discovered, he was still out there somewhere. He may have even gotten a look at who shot him. Koblanski pushed that thought from his mind, choosing, instead, to embrace the optimistic notion that Townes had been too distracted with staying alive to notice who shot him. And if that were the case, Koblanski thought, he needed to start looking for someone to buy the Brooklyn Bridge from him, because he was the luckiest pollock in the world.

Between the men he had standing guard at

Bamma Brooks's hospital room, the ones scouring the city for Townes, and those making sure Red Linny's operation moved smoothly, Koblanski had a plate full of mashed potatoes and bullshit, with not nearly enough mashed potatoes. For the first time in his crooked career as one of New York City's finest, Stan Koblanski worried about getting caught. Hell, he hadn't even worried about the fucking idiot mayor and his Knapp Commission, that's how well protected he was within the force. But all this business with Red Linny had him crapping his pants and considering early retirement.

Koblankski worked uptown most of his career, and knew the ins and outs of dealing with crime and criminals in Harlem. It didn't matter if it was the guineas on the eastside decades ago, or the spades and spics that now called the shots, Koblanski knew how to keep everyone in line. That wasn't the case, however, with Red Linny Morton. Aside from the fact that Morton was a complete psychopath, he had connections with real power. Koblanski couldn't prove it, but his suspicions pointed toward federal connections. The city was lousy with undercover assholes working for the Bureau of Narcotics and the FBI, making it so that any cop—corrupt or otherwise—had trouble doing their job.

Koblankski didn't have proof of Red Linny's connection to someone in some federal bureau, but he knew it existed. Men like Morton didn't wield this kind of power unless it had been bestowed on them from somewhere further up the food chain. Morton had his hands in dope and weapons—both in the kind of volume that meant his connections weren't playing around. Throw in the fact that Red Linny had popped up practically from nowhere, and it meant he was a player in a much bigger game.

Morton had done time as a juvenile, and at seventeen had been tried and convicted as an adult. If it hadn't been for his clubbed foot, he might've avoid prison and gone to Vietnam, but no such luck. Koblanski had reviewed the files he could find on Morton, but there wasn't much to explain how he had become the sort of guy that made others piss their pants. Something happened between 1962, when seventeen year-old Linwood Morton went to prison, and 1967, when he got out and started building his own unique crime empire. More specifically, someone must have come along—a fellow inmate with the right outside contacts—who got Morton started down his path. Koblanksi didn't know who that person was, nor did he care to know, but he knew they existed just the same.

Koblanski pulled his car to the curb at a vacant spot on Lenox Avenue, three blocks from Harlem

Hospital. He walked past a patrol car parked in front of the hospital as he tried to figure out how to get himself out of the current situation that only threatened to get worse.

For starters, he needed to take care of Bamma Brooks. Technically, Brooks was Morton's problem—his loose thread to deal with. Koblanski knew, however, that some loose threads were big enough to hang more than one person, and he wasn't about to let this become one of those threads.

After taking care of Brooks, he needed to find Harry Townes and eliminate him. Once that had been taken care of, Koblanski would put in his retirement papers and get out while the getting was good. Along the way, he might have to get rid of Red Linny, which didn't bother him.

He felt a sense of calm, realizing that as bad as things were—as much as he felt like he was in over his head—he could still have his happy ending. Sure, his happy ending meant some people had to die, but that's how things were—as long as he wasn't one of the dead ones, everything would be fine.

# TWENTY-SEVEN

"Good evening, We Don't Sleep So You Can, how can I help you?"

"John Shaft." He didn't recognize the voice of the receptionist. She sounded younger than most of the other women who worked at the answering service, who lived their lives as disembodied voices taking messages for other people.

"Good evening, Mr. Shaft. Only one message for you. A woman named April called at 8:15, and wanted you to know that your friend is doing better."

"Thanks," said Shaft. He decided that this receptionist was a young co-ed, working her way through college.

"That's good news, right?" asked the receptionist.

"Pardon me?"

"That your friend is feeling better. That's good news, right?"

"Better than the alternative," said Shaft, before

thanking the receptionist.

He hung up the receiver of the pay phone, checked to see if by some miracle the dime he'd deposited had somehow been refunded to him—not that they ever were, but he could hope. He checked his watch, and realized he'd passed the twenty-four hour mark of no sleep.

April Carmichael had left a message, which meant he wouldn't be getting any sleep in the immediate future. April was a nurse up at Harlem Hospital. She was one of the few women Shaft knew socially that he hadn't slept with. Not that he didn't want to; it had just never worked out that way. Maybe April reminded him too much of Arletha—someone who was too good for him. He had trouble with women like that— he didn't want them getting too close, and then leaving behind a void he could never fill. He'd long since realized that he couldn't bring Arletha back from the dead, no matter how much he fucked, and didn't want to go through that again. And so the good women—the women like April—remained friends. At least as much as Shaft was friends with any woman.

Shaft asked April to keep a discreet eye on Bamma Brooks. He didn't want her doing anything that might arouse suspicion, but at the same time he wanted to make sure he had some idea of Brooks's status. He didn't owe anything to Brooks—they'd been squared up for a long time. Still, Shaft knew that he was tied to the gangster the same way he was tied to Harry Townes, bound together by a dead man who'd hired Shaft from beyond the grave. They were all members of the same fraternity—a brotherhood of men shot because of their association with Knocks Persons.

Anderozzi had dropped Shaft off in the Bronx, on his way to take Townes someplace safe. Shaft didn't ask the location of this safe place, nor did he want to know. Shaft, Townes, and Anderozzi were now comrades in arms, for better or worse, yet all three recognized the need to play some cards close to the chest. Whatever place Townes was going to go as he planned his next move was one of those cards.

Shaft parted company with his companions, letting them know he planned on following up on leads of his own, and all three agreeing to touch base within the next few hours. Shaft had planned to return to his office and check out the remaining contents of the box Knocks Persons had left for him. On a whim, however, he decided to check his messages, a hunch that had paid off.

He caught a gypsy cab—the only kind he could find in the Bronx past midnight—instructing the driver to take Jerome Avenue south until it led to Macomb's Dam Bridge and crossed over into Harlem.

"There's quicker ways to get to Harlem," said the

driver.

"I ain't in no hurry, and I need time to think," said Shaft, handing the driver two twenty-dollar bills. "And don't worry about red lights."

Shaft would use this slightly longer route to catch a quick nap in the back of the cab. This had become a regular routine for him, as he'd discovered that there was something restful and calming about being in a cab—provided, of course, he kept his eyes closed and tuned out everything around him. The fact of the matter was that he'd caught a few minutes of much needed sleep in places far more improbable than the back of a taxicab.

The driver dropped Shaft off around the corner from Harlem Hospital. Shaft had no reason for extra precaution, except for the fact that he was swimming upstream in a river of shit, and that always seemed to call for added precaution, if not downright paranoia. A police car sat parked in front of the hospital.

Visiting hours had ended, not that such things mattered in this case. Bamma Brooks had armed policemen guarding his room, and Shaft's precautious paranoia told him that chances were good the cops watching the room were of the crooked variety. Either way, he wasn't going to be able to waltz into the room.

Getting close to Brooks would require equal parts cunning and stealth, with a likely amount of shuck-

and-jive. Shaft entered the hospital unnoticed. For all anyone who may have seen him knew, he was just another orderly, showing up late for his shift.

First, Shaft found a supply closet, where he grabbed surgical scrubs big enough to fit over his clothes. The light blue clothing fit loosely over his street clothes, but still felt somewhat binding. Not that comfort mattered. Shaft just needed to look like maybe, somehow, he belonged in a hospital at this late hour.

Walking with his head hung low, hoping no one noticed him, he found another janitorial supply closet. The surgical scrubs allowed him to look like he might belong, but he couldn't risk being mistaken for someone important. He needed to blend in innocuously.

Inside the janitorial supply closet, he found a mop and a bucket that he proceeded to fill with water. His improvised undercover outfit was a joke—surgical scrubs and a mop and bucket. But Shaft knew from past experience that a black man with a mop and bucket could go damn near anywhere, and no one ever asked any questions—even if he was dressed in surgical scrubs. The low expectations set for black men in America was a form of damnation—a fate akin to being locked in a tiny cell, with a ceiling so low you couldn't stand upright. But sometimes those low expectations made it easier to go places you weren't supposed to go.

April Carmichael had already given Shaft the room number for Bamma Brooks. The private detective stepped off the elevator, pushing the bucket and mop down a long corridor, turned the corner, and stopped short when he saw the uniformed police officer standing outside a room talking to another man.

Shaft assumed the other man to be Koblanski, largely based on the ill-fitting suit that betrayed him as being a plainclothes cop. He didn't know Koblanski by sight, but Shaft did know a corrupt cop when he saw one. Everything about corrupt cops was different, from the way they walked to the way they talked. They stood a certain way—had a body language that was unique to them and them alone. Even corrupt cops in uniform had the same posture that identified them as a different kind of predatory pig. Shaft knew this particular species of swine all too well—one had nearly cracked his skull open ten years earlier.

Shaft mopped the floor, keeping his head low to avoid any possibility of recognition. He hummed to himself as part of his disguise, while he strained to hear the conversation between the uniformed officer and the man in the polyester business suit. At this distance, Shaft couldn't hear anything. But he could see the face of the uniformed cop. He could see the way the man in uniform held himself—the tension on his face, the way he clenched and unclenched his fists, the beads of sweat on his furrowed brow glistening in the fluorescent light of the hallway. Shaft knew that the cop was being given the kill order. He'd seen enough men respond to that order that he recognized it the way some people recognized storm clouds while others only saw clouds.

Inching closer, taking great care to mop the floor as he moved forward, Shaft's mind raced. He had hoped to sneak in to see Bamma Brooks under the pretense of mopping the floor—not exactly the best plan in the first place, and maybe getting a few words out of him. Instead, his precautious paranoia told him he'd arrived just as Brooks was to be silenced forever.

Before Shaft could get close enough to hear anything, the man he believed to be Koblanski walked off. Koblanski—or whoever he was—never even looked at Shaft as he strolled past. Shaft, however, got a good look at him, cautiously watching as the poorly dressed man with the gait of a corrupt cop walked down the hall, and turned the corner heading off toward the elevator.

Shaft looked back toward the room, seeing that the uniformed cop was no longer standing outside. Shaft rushed toward the room, pushing the mop and bucket with him, just in case he still needed his disguise. Just in case he was simply being paranoid, and found himself looking for an explanation as to why he'd barged into a patient's room.

The cop had a pillow placed over Bamma Brooks's face. The weakened gangster struggled in vain as the police officer pressed down with his entire body, smothering the life from Brooks. The cop turned, looking surprised at the janitor dressed in hospital scrubs.

"What the fuck…?" he mumbled, before being cut off by Shaft.

Shaft leapt across the room, slamming into the cop and knocking him off Brooks. The cop let out a gasp as he crashed to the floor, Shaft landing on top of him.

Shaft and the cop began to wrestle on the floor. The officer reached for his gun, but Shaft managed to knock it from the cop's hand. Whatever element of surprise that may have given Shaft the upper hand in the fight disappeared. The two men struggled, the cop pushing Shaft off him, giving both men time to get on their feet.

"You're dead, nigger," growled the cop.

He pulled out his nightstick, taking a swing at Shaft in the cramped quarters of the hospital room. Shaft moved out of the way of the nightstick, grabbed the mop, and used it to block a second swing from the cop. Shaft smashed the officer in the face with the wet dirty head of the mop.

The blow did little to hurt the officer, but it humiliated him, pushing him into a blind range. He rushed forward like a football player, slamming into Shaft's torso, and knocking him into the bathroom.

Shaft felt a shooting pain in his back, as he slammed into the sink in the bathroom. He grabbed the back of the officer's head, and brought his knee up to connect with the cop's face. A crunch let Shaft know he'd broken the officer's nose, which erupted in blood.

The sight of his own blood sent the cop into a frenzied rage. He swung his fists like a wild animal having a seizure. The cop's fist connected with Shaft's jaw, sending the private detective to the floor.

The cop kicked at Shaft, but Shaft grabbed the officer's leg and held on, making it impossible to kick anymore. Shaft realized he was in a terrible position, the result of a punch landing with blind luck.

Shaft needed to get on his feet—fast—before the sound of the fight brought unwanted attention, or before the cop got lucky, and ended everything. Shaft struggled to get up off the floor, while the cop tried to kick with his free leg. Neither man could get into a tactically advantageous position in the tiny bathroom. Fighting in a room as small as the hospital bathroom was as awkward and cramped as screwing in the backseat of a Volkswagen Beetle.

The cop stooped down and started throwing

punches as Shaft, whose arms were wrapped around his attacker's leg.

"Fuckin' motherfucker," said the cop. "I'm gonna…"

His words were cut short by a loud metal clank. The cop stumbled forward, slamming into the plastic door of the shower stall, and giving Shaft the precious few seconds he needed to get back on his feet.

Shaft grabbed the cop from behind. The cop drove his elbow into Shaft's torso, hard enough to be felt, but not felt as anything more than an irritation.

Holding on to the back of the police officer's shirt collar, Shaft slammed the cop head first into the shower door. The force of the blow smashed the door off its chrome hinges, but didn't do enough to end the fight.

Gripping the cop's collar, Shaft whipped the man around, slamming the officer's head into the sink with a sickening thunk. With less give than the plastic shower door, the porcelain sink proved to be the immovable object Shaft needed against the irresistible force of the cop, who dropped to the floor, unconscious.

His heart pounding, his breathing labored, Shaft looked up to see Bamma Brooks, standing on wobbly legs, like a fighter who'd gone fifteen rounds, but should've only lasted ten. Brooks clutched a metal bedpan with a dent in the bottom in his hands.

"That honky motherfucker tried to kill me," croaked Brooks, his voice weak and unsteady.

Shaft helped Brooks back to the bed.

Shaft needed a plan, yet he had none. He needed to think fast, and move with a swiftness that eluded most people. This swiftness was a combination of thought and action, bound together so tightly it was impossible to know where one ended and the other began. It came naturally to Shaft, who first learned he possessed this ability when he was a kid in Harlem. He sharpened the skills in the boxing ring, and then perfected them in the jungles of Vietnam. Others had tested his skills—his ability to survive—and while they had left scars on him, Shaft had left them dead.

"We gotta get the fuck outta here," said Shaft.

"Can't walk, kid. Too weak," said Brooks.

"I got it," said Shaft, hurrying out of the room.

A few minutes later, he returned to the room with a wheelchair. Shaft helped Brooks into the chair, shot a glance back at the cop lying on the bathroom floor, blood pouring from his broken nose. The detective's mind raced as he looked over at the cop lying on the floor. He didn't even know if the cop was alive or dead. If the pig was dead, Shaft was screwed—though it meant a quick getaway. And if the cop wasn't dead, Shaft was screwed as soon as the officer regained consciousness.

Shaft stepped into the bathroom, stooped down, and found the cop's pulse. Without appearing to give it any thought, he removed the radio from the cop's belt and tossed it to Brooks—no calling for back up. He then stuffed a towel into the officer's mouth, and tied the gag in place using I.V. tubing—no screaming for help. He fished around the cops pockets for keys, tossing those to Brooks as well. Finally, Shaft used to the cop's handcuffs to chain the officer to the sink in the bathroom, with his hands behind his back—no pulling out the gag. This would buy Shaft and Brooks some time.

Shaft turned off the light in the bathroom, closed the door so no one would see the cop right away. He wheeled Brooks down the hall, to the elevator, and out a side exit. He pushed the wheelchair toward the patrol car parked outside the hospital, hoping it was the ride of the man he'd left chained to the sink upstairs.

The key fit in the door lock. With Bamma Brooks in the passenger seat, John Shaft pulled away from the curb in front of Harlem Hospital in a stolen police car.

"Remind me to never fuck with you," said Brooks, his voice weak.

"Never Fuck With Me is my middle name," said Shaft.

Brooks laughed at the joke—a reminder of his old boss, Junius Tate.

"First time you ever steal a car?" asked Brooks.

"First time I've stolen a cop car," said Shaft. "But I gotta be honest, in the broad scheme of things, being in a stolen cop car is the least of my concerns."

Shaft's mind still raced. He had no idea where to go next—what to do next. If he'd been swimming upstream in a river of shit before, the current had swept him out to sea, and now he was drowning. He thought of the bodies he'd seen fall into the Saigon River, only to be carried out to the East Sea, and for the first time since he'd come back from the war, Shaft found himself in a situation that made him wish he was back in Vietnam.

# TWENTY-EIGHT

Vic Anderozzi turned his car onto University Avenue in the Bronx and checked his rearview mirror for what had to be the millionth time. As he navigated his way through Harlem, Anderozzi had been pretty sure he'd picked up a tail. Now that he'd made it to the Bronx, he felt it with a certainty in his gut.

He didn't know exactly when they'd been made—or how—but it must've happened when he dropped off Shaft. Or maybe someone had spotted Harry Townes in the backseat. Hell, for all Anderozzi knew, they may have been made back when they crossed over the George Washington Bridge. It didn't really matter. The only thing that mattered was that he and Townes were being tailed, like they were the bad guys.

Crooked cops had targeted Townes. Shaft may have been targeted as well. And because he'd helped them, Vic Anderozzi now had a target on his back, and an unmarked cop car tailing him in the Bronx.

"How you doing back there?" Anderozzi asked.

Townes sat in the backseat, leaning against the door. His body screamed at him to lie down, but he refused to give in. "Feel like shit," mumbled Townes.

"Well, maybe this will cheer you up," Anderozzi said. "We've got someone on our ass."

Townes wanted to turn around to see if he could spot the tail, but that required too much energy. "Of course we do," he said. He tried to laugh, but the muscles required refused to respond, as if they failed to see the humor in an ever worsening situation.

"You got your piece?" Anderozzi asked.

Townes weakly moved his hand to the holster on his belt. He could feel his gun, but worried if he had the strength to hold it, let alone fire it. "I got it. But the shape I'm in, I couldn't fire straight to save my life."

"I don't give a shit if you can shoot straight—just so long as you don't hit me," said Anderozzi. He pulled to a stop at a yellow light. He checked the rearview mirror. Whoever was following him was three cars back. The light in front of him turned red, and Anderozzi mashed down on the gas, taking off like a rocket through the intersection. Cars to his left and right slammed on their brakes to avoid slamming into him.

"What the fuck're you doing?" asked Townes.

"Seeing how bad they want you."

Townes felt a sense of dread course through his weakened body. He removed his gun from the holster. "How bad?" he asked.

Anderozzi shifted his gaze from the road ahead to the rearview mirror. Oncoming headlights cut through the intersection, narrowly avoiding being hit. If he'd had any doubts about being followed, they'd been dismissed. "Pretty fuckin' bad," said Anderozzi.

Townes shifted his body, letting out a groan of pain as he looked out the back window. The car chasing them was less than half a block away, and closing fast. "What're we doing?" he asked.

"Not really sure. I'm used to chasing, not being chased," Anderozzi said. The severity of their situation swept over him like a tidal wave as he floored the gas pedal. Cops were chasing him and Townes. They were being hunted by those that were supposed to be their brothers-in-arms. The only problem was that the pursuers were in league with whoever had already tried to kill Townes.

Anderozzi had no illusions about bad cops on the force. At the end of the day, cops were people too, and there were plenty of bad people in the world. The difference between knowing that there were dangerously corrupt cops and actually dealing with them were two completely different things. One was an exercise in pragmatism, the other an exercise in survival. One was a conversation you had; the other was making a decision about potentially killing someone else—about killing another cop.

It dawned on Anderozzi that sometime in the next few minutes, he was likely to be killed by another cop, or he might have to do the killing. His heart raced as his adrenaline pumped.

"Put on your seatbelt," said Anderozzi.

"What?" asked Townes.

"Buckle up," said Anderozzi, strapping himself in. "This is going to hurt."

He eased up on the gas a bit—just enough for the other car to get dangerously close. Then Vic Anderozzi slammed on the brakes.

The pursuing car barely had time to slow down before crashing into Anderozzi. And even then, the pursuers hadn't slowed down enough.

The force of the collision violently jerked Anderozzi and Townes. Had it not been for their seatbelts, they'd have been thrown from the car.

The driver of the car behind them wasn't so lucky. His body shot from the front seat like a cannonball, smashing through the windshield, and crashing into the rear window of Anderozzi's car. He never felt the impact of his face on the rear window, as his neck had snapped the moment he was ejected from his own ride.

Anderozzi climbed out of his car, his body screaming in pain from the force of impact, his head bleeding from being smashed against the steering wheel. His adrenaline allowed him to ignore the pain—or at least not give in to it as he stumbled over to the other car.

He recognized the passenger of the other car, though he couldn't remember the other detective's name. Anderozzi checked the other cop for a pulse. When he found it, he fought the urge to put a bullet through the man's skull. Instead, he opened the car door, undid the man's seatbelt, and dragged him out of the car.

The other cop let out a grunt of pain as his body hit the ground.

"You need help?"

Anderozzi looked over to see Townes, leaning against the side of the car.

"I got this," said Anderozzi. He looked down at the unconscious cop lying at his feet. He had to get the corrupt piece of shit into the back of his car, and there was no time to spare. He started to drag the body to his car.

Townes helped Anderozzi stuff the unconscious cop into the back of the car, but not before they handcuffed the man.

Anderozzi got back behind the steering wheel, while Townes sat next to him in the passenger's seat.

The dead body of the other driver rolled off the back of the car and hit the ground as Anderozzi drove away. Townes started to laugh.

"What's so fuckin' funny?" asked Anderozzi.

"I was just thinking," said Townes. "I hope Shaft is having better luck than us."

# TWENTY-NINE

Shaft seldom felt fear. He felt concern. He felt apprehension. He calculated and acted with caution, planning his moves with precision and confidence that left no time or place for fear. Fear got you caught or killed when freedom and staying alive were the only objectives. John Shaft had learned long ago how to control his fears—a control that kept him out of prison and drawing breath. But driving around Harlem in a stolen police car, with a targeted gangster as his passenger, and not a shred of a plan of where to go or what to do, left Shaft feeling fear like he'd never felt before. The Grim Reaper might as well have been in the passenger seat next to him, giving him directions to Hell.

Bamma Brooks mumbled the address of some place on 138th, near Striver's Row. Shaft didn't ask specifics. He didn't need to know where he was going, because having some place to go was good enough.

Shaft turned the police cruiser off Adam Clayton Powell Boulevard and onto 138th, pulling the car to the curb in front of an aging brownstone halfway down the block. It looked no different from any of the other structures lining the street, though Shaft suspected this place to be different.

Five men came out of the building, dressed a bit too nice for the time of night. Shaft recognized none of them, but he knew their vocation. They were all gangsters, dressed in stylish suits that were only worn by men with power. It didn't matter if that power came with the financial means to make or break people, or if it came with a loaded gun and not giving a fuck enough to keep from using it.

Shaft wondered how the men had spotted them in the car so quickly. There must've been a lookout somewhere along the way that they'd passed—someone whose job it was to keep an eye open for trouble. Maybe this person had simply spotted the cop car, or maybe they'd actually seen Shaft and Brooks. Either way, a call had been made, and a greeting party had been put together.

Three of the men helped Brooks out of the car, all but carrying him inside the brownstone. One of the other men took Shaft's place behind the wheel of the cop car, taking off without a word. Shaft watched the car pull off, admiring the efficiency of the operation.

He held his arms up and off to the side, offering no protest as the fifth man patted him down. Shaft expected no less from whomever it was he and Brooks had dropped by to see at this late hour.

"This way," said the fifth man.

"Where's he taking the ride?" Shaft asked, following the man up the front stoop.

"Why you ask?" growled the man. His voice was deep—his accent distinctly southern.

"Case I ever need to ditch a hot cop car again."

The fifth man let out a sound that might have been a laugh—a deep, muffled "hurumph," which was the best you could ever hope to get from someone paid to inflict pain.

Shaft followed the man down a long hallway into a parlor with high ceilings. An old man sat in the room, wearing white gloves and dressed in a suit that cost more than most people in Harlem made in a month. Even the chair looked expensive, like the descendant of European thrones upon which many a royal ass had sat.

The room looked like a museum exhibit of the Harlem that had once been. On one of the walls hung framed photos of Harlem's who's who, and standing next to every musician, politician, and athlete was the old man sitting on the chair of royalty across from Shaft. In the pictures, the man was much younger, but still recognizable, with his high cheek bones, angular nose, and trademark white gloves. All of these photos spoke of a man that had rubbed shoulders with the best and brightest. The other pictures, however, told the tale of a man that had stood next to the most dangerous and deadly.

Along with the photos of Count Bassie, Billie Holiday, Malcolm X, and Joe Louis, there were pictures of Knocks Persons, Bumpy Johnson, Queenie St. Claire, and dozens of other notorious Harlem crime figures. These photos spoke more clearly and loudly to Shaft than the snapshots of celebrities and politicians. The candid nature of the pictures, the smiles and familiarity let Shaft know that he sat in the company of someone big and important, or at least someone who once had been both. And in all the photos, the man wore white gloves. Shaft wondered who the old man could possibly be, though two pictures in particular gave him clues.

The first picture was of the old man when he was much younger. Standing next to him was none other than Josiah "Bluehand Geechie" Moseley, one of Harlem's most legendary gangsters. Every kid in Harlem knew Bluehand Geechie, just like they knew Queenie St. Claire, and Bumpy Johnson. They were all members of the Forty Thieves, which stood up to the Italian mob to take control of Harlem.

The second photo was also of the old man, many years earlier, standing next to two other young black men, all three of them dressed in the best fashions of the day. Shaft recognized two of the men in the picture as Isaac and Elijah Moseley—the notorious Moseley Twins, sons of Bluehand Geechie. Growing up, Shaft had heard plenty of stories about the Moseley Twins, also members of the Forty Thieves. The Moseleys had a younger brother, and Shaft wondered if that was who now sat across from him—Moses Moseley, the last of Harlem's old guard, son of Bluehand Geechie.

Shaft rolled the idea around in his head. It made sense. Moses Moseley was an enigma, seldom seen in public, known more for his reclusive nature than the flamboyant lifestyle attributed to so many other gangsters. The old man sitting across from Shaft was the right age to be the youngest of Bluehand Geechie's sons—the son who inherited the family empire, consolidating everything into Harlem's most successful loan shark operation. He invested wisely, in a real estate and a funeral home, retiring early from a life of crime. Most telling about the old man, however, were the white gloves. Rumor had it that Moses Moseley always wore white gloves, so his hands wouldn't be stained by the work he did. The hands of his father had been stained blue from a childhood of slaving away at giant vats of indigo dye.

Shaft had never seen Moses Moseley in real life. Cookie Venable and Red Linny both claimed they had seen the gangster, and Shaft took them at their word. He also never doubted the stories of Moses always wearing white gloves to keep his hands clean. The more he thought about it, the more he became convinced that the man sitting across from him was the son of Bluehand Geechie.

One of the men that helped carry Bamma Brooks from the car into the house entered the room. He leaned in close and whispered something into the old man's ear. Shaft couldn't make out anything being said. The old man didn't verbally respond, he just nodded his head like a silent king whose orders need not be spoken aloud.

The hired muscle left the room, headed on a mission of some sort, and the old man looked over at Shaft.

"You know me," said the old man, no intonation of inquiry in his voice. He wasn't asking a question, so much as he was issuing a demand.

Shaft studied the old man. He had to be close to ninety—if not older. This man, in his white gloves, had been around at the turn of the century. He'd been raised by former slaves, and seen all the marvels of the twentieth century when they were still new. Even at this advanced age, the man's posture showed no sign of the world weariness that made men half his age slump over. His eyes still burned with the rarest of fires—the fire of a black man that hadn't been broken by the system.

"Moses Moseley," said Shaft. He said it with the confidence and respect reserved for few people.

The old man nodded his head slightly, a smile creeping across his face, as if the sound of his own name made him happy. Or maybe he was just happy that someone recognized him after all these years—that his reputation endured, while the kingdom he once ruled collapsed into decay all around him. "Guess what they say about you is true," said Moseley.

Shaft shrugged his shoulders. "As true as what they say about you," said Shaft.

"Done good, boy," said Moseley. "Bamma survives all this, he owes you more than he owes me, and he owes me a lot."

Shaft nodded. "You getting him to doctor?" he asked.

"Gettin' him outta town first. No safe place around here. He live long enough to get outta here, he'll be fine. "

"If he lives," Shaft said.

"That countrified negro been through worse shit than this. 'Sides, no one lives forever. Might just be God and the Devil decided it were time to see who gets to spend eternity with that tough sumbitch." Moseley laughed, picturing the argument over possession of Bamma Brooks's soul.

"Could be," said Shaft.

"Lotta bad shit goin' down in Harlem—but you already know that. Never thought anyone would take out Knocks," said Moseley. "Shit, only reason they ain't come for me is because I'm out the game so long."

"Looks to me like you're still calling shots."

"I got money, and I got family around to protect me. That ain't the same as being in the game."

"You've got enough to take care of Brooks," said Shaft.

"Brooks is kinfolk—that's why I'm helping. My third wife and his mama are sisters. That makes him family. Sooner or later, this shit will bite me in the ass," said Moseley. "Now, tell me what done happened, boy."

Shaft recounted everything that had happened after he arrived at the hospital. Hearing the words coming from his mouth, it all sounded so unbelievable—even for Shaft. Maybe Anderozzi was right. Maybe he was a shit magnet.

"Rode off into the night in the cop's car. That's the special magic, boy," said Moseley, a devilish grin creeping across his face. "That's the kinda magic make yo' daddy proud."

"Excuse me?" Shaft asked, uncertain of the old

man's meaning.

"I said yo' daddy be proud, he see the kinda magic you got. He hated him some police. He most certainly did. 'Spose that's something y'all have in common."

Shaft winced at the mention of his father. It felt like a raw nerve had been touched with a hot blade. No one ever talked about his father, and Shaft knew nothing of the man. His father had been killed before Shaft was two years old—he had no memories of the man. Had never even seen a picture.

"What're you talkin' about?" Shaft asked. The tone in his voice betrayed his emotions.

Moses Moseley stared into the eyes of John Shaft, and he saw a truth that couldn't be hidden. Shaft was like too many of the boys on the streets of Harlem— fatherless, with no memories to guide them through life. These boys became men that defined manhood on their own terms, leaving behind the sad child that longed to have a father. They traded their abandonment and loneliness for the trappings of what it meant to be a man—at least a perception of what it meant to be a man.

"Your daddy—Quick Johnny—he was a good man," said Moses.

Shaft felt like a grenade had gone off inside his gut. He felt a rush of emotion like he'd never felt before— not even after he'd found the love of his life murdered in her apartment. "Quick Johnny?" whispered Shaft.

Questions raced through Shaft's brain—so many things to ask, and no idea where to start. All he knew about his father was the name listed on his birth certificate—John Quentin Smith—and the rumor he'd been a numbers runner. Shaft's parents had never been married, and his mother gave her only son her last name. If she ever talked about his father before she died when Shaft was three, he had no memory of it. Hell, he had only a few memories of her. If his mother was nothing more than a ghost, his father was the shadow of a ghost. In the word-of-mouth lore that passed for history on the streets, Shaft's father had his throat slit over a numbers dispute.

"You knew my father?" asked Shaft.

"Shit, boy, everyone knew your daddy. Quick Johnny Smith was the baddest nigger in Harlem. And before that, he was the baddest motherfucker in San Juan Hill."

Shaft fought to make sense of everything, but there was no sense to be found. There were no answers—at least not any answers that he had. There was so much he wanted to know—so much he wanted to ask. He didn't even know where to begin. Lost in the flood of emotions and questions, Shaft came crashing back to reality as the sound of machine gun fire erupted outside the house of Moses Moseley. They were under attack.

# THIRTY

Shaft sprang into action. He moved across the room, grabbing Moses Moseley and pulling him to the floor. Shaft hoped the old man's aging bones could withstand the impact of hitting the floor, which seemed far better than taking a hit from a bullet.

Shaft twisted in mid air, so that his body hit the floor first. Shaft grunted under the double impact of dropping to the floor and then having the weight of Moseley crash down on him a fraction of a second later.

The sound of gunfire and shattering glass filled the front of the brownstone, as Shaft scanned the room for cover. This far into the house they were only so safe, and that didn't factor in the attackers storming the house. Shaft's mind flashed back to Knocks Persons's home—the killers had come into the house.

Two of Moseley's hired muscle raced into the parlor, crouched down low, weapons in their hands. "You alright, poppa?" shouted one of the men.

"Get those motherfuckers!" shouted Moseley.

One of the musclemen moved in close. "No, sir. Gotta get you outta here."

Only then did Shaft see the resemblance between the two bodyguards and Moseley. These weren't mob enforcers, they were either sons or grandsons of Moseley.

"You got an extra gun?" Shaft asked.

One of the men pulled an extra .45 automatic from a shoulder holster under his jacket and handed it to Shaft.

"Don't know what you got in mind as far as escape plans, but whatever it is, get ready to do it," said Shaft.

Crouching low, Shaft moved out of the parlor and into the long hallway leading to the front entrance of the brownstone. The non-stop gunfire from outside had tapered off into a series of short, controlled bursts. For every burst of machine gun fire coming from outside, a series of shots came from several handguns on the inside.

Moseley had just the right amount of men required for an aging, retired gangster—enough men to make him feel safe, but not enough to protect him from the M16 onslaught tearing up the front of his home.

It made no sense to Shaft. *Why the fuck would any-*

*one come after Moseley? He's so old, he farts dust.*

Down low, pressing up against the wall as much as possible, Shaft moved closer to the front of the house. All the lights had been shot out, making it difficult to see in the darkness. As he moved, it dawned on Shaft with a grim certainty—a stark realization that slammed into him with more weight than the old man falling on top of him back in the parlor. *The gunmen outside aren't after Moseley, they're after me and Brooks.*

Just as Moseley had someone on lookout somewhere near the house, there had to have been another set of eyes watching. Someone must've known that Brooks would turn to Moseley in times of trouble. That someone had probably been watching the house for more than a week. It was likely part of the reason Moseley never visited Brooks in the hospital.

Shaft reached the end of the hallway where the landing of the stairs met with the front foyer. One of Moseley's men had taken a defensive position close to the front door. Another one of the men lay sprawled out on the floor.

"Hey," Shaft called out in a loud whisper. "How many?"

"Three or four. Got one trying to get inside. Think we scared 'em away."

"No. They're just regrouping since one of 'em went down. Any minute now, they'll storm the place," Shaft said, inching closer to the landing of the stairs. "Count to sixty, then lay down some fire to get their attention. Only enough to get their attention. Then crawl on your belly back to the old man."

Shaft bounded up the stairs, hoping no one outside had noticed him. He reached the top landing of the second floor and raced over to the small mezzanine that looked out over the front of the brownstone. From downstairs he heard three gunshots, followed by a volley of returned fire from outside. Muzzle flashes identified Shaft's three targets.

Shaft squeezed off four rounds, taking out two of his targets, before the third leapt out of the way, simultaneously firing up into the second floor mezzanine window. Dropping back, Shaft scurried back to the stairs and down to the first floor foyer. He paused at the bullet-riddled front door for a brief moment, listening to the machine gun blasting outside. The gunman was still firing up toward the second floor.

Shaft whipped the front door open, lining up his target before the gunmen even had a chance to redirect the spray of his weapon. Shaft let loose a single shot into the head of the gunman, trying to ignore the fact that at a quick glance his victim looked shockingly young.

Cautiously moving to the front steps, Shaft grabbed a machine gun from the hands of a dead gunman at the top of the stoop. He quickly scanned the outside area for other would-be assassins, or oncoming police—not that there was a difference. He saw nothing, but knew that either or both were only moments away.

Shaft turned his attention back into the brownstone. "Coast is clear!" shouted Shaft. "Get the fuck outta here, now!"

A flurry of movement filled the hallway as Moses Moseley was hustled by his family toward an open door leading to a second staircase, descending to the basement.

Shaft moved quickly toward the second staircase, never taking his eyes off the front door. He pulled the door to the basement staircase closed behind him, bolting down the steps, hot on the heels of Moseley and the others.

The basement was a cramped deathtrap—the worst place anyone could have chosen to run from a gunfight. Moseley was there with his remaining bodyguards, along with Bamma Brooks, who couldn't stand on his feet without help from someone else. They all looked like trapped rats, waiting to be killed. Shaft started to curse whoever thought the basement was a good place to hide. He held his tongue as he saw one of the bodyguards pull a hidden lever on the far back wall, activating a sliding door.

On the other side of the door was a giant hidden room—a holdover from another time. Maybe it had once been a speakeasy during the days of prohibition, or a secret gambling den. Harlem was littered with secret rooms just like this one.

Shaft stepped into the secret room, and one of the bodyguards slid the door shut behind him. Moseley and his other men were already at the far end of the secret room, and another hidden passageway had been opened. Shaft helped the lone bodyguard trying to keep Brooks on his feet. Together they moved into a corridor that stretched for at least one hundred yards, before curving off to the left.

"How you doin'?" Shaft asked Brooks.

"Don't think I can make it, kid," Brooks said. His words came out weak.

"Die on your own time, man. Not mine," growled Shaft.

Shaft, Brooks, and the third man struggled to move down the narrow passageway. They moved slowly, having to pause every few seconds because of Brooks. Up ahead, Moseley and the others disappeared from sight.

"Fuck this," said Shaft. "I got him."

Shaft handed the machine gun to the other man. He crouched down, and scooped Brooks up in a fireman's lift, slinging the injured gangster on his shoulders. Shaft let out a strained grunt—it felt like his back would break from the added weight. Many years had passed since Shaft carried another man this way, and then it had been in a jungle. Shaft broke out into a jog, the bodyguard following behind him.

The passageway curved to the left, leading to a staircase. Shaft took care maneuvering up the stairs—making sure he didn't smash Brooks's head. The top of the stairs opened up into the backroom of a corner market.

Moseley and two of his men stood in the darkness of the store. Shaft squatted down to get Brooks from off his back, while the others helped Brooks stay on his feet.

"Thanks," said Brooks.

"I hope there's a plan," said Shaft.

"Don't get to be my age without having a plan," said Moseley.

A car pulled up outside the store. Shaft immediately reached for the .45 automatic tucked into the waist of his pants.

Moseley held up his hand, stopping Shaft from moving into action. "It's okay, boy," said Moseley. The old man looked Shaft up and down. "Yeah, you really are Quick Johnny's boy."

Shaft wanted to ask Moseley a million questions, but there was no time. He helped Brooks makes his way to the car parked outside the store. One of the bodyguard's sat behind the wheel of a giant Cadillac.

Moses Moseley slid into the backseat. "You comin' with us, boy?" the old man asked.

"No," said Shaft, helping Brooks get into the backseat. "Too much shit to do."

Brooks looked up at Shaft from the backseat of the car. One of the toughest men Shaft had ever known looked weak and frail. "Gotta tell you something," said Brooks.

"What's that?" Shaft asked.

"I know who killed Knocks—saw the motherfucker come up outta the basement," said Brooks. "It was that hi-yella nigger you used to run with—the one with the fucked up eyes and the limp."

"What..." Shaft struggled to find the words. Before he could regain his thoughts, the Cadillac pulled off, leaving Shaft alone, and more confused than he'd ever been in his life.

There had to be a mistake. Brooks didn't know what the fuck he was talking about. There was no way the killer of Knocks Persons was Red Linny Morton—one of Shaft's best childhood friends.

# THIRTY-ONE

The decision to kill Knocks Persons came easily to Red Linny Morton. After the death of Bumpy Johnson, it had been business as usual in Harlem, with Persons rising to power as the undisputed kingpin. This all happened with Red Linny still locked up in Attica. And if Knocks hadn't had the change of heart—hadn't felt the need to redeem himself over some misplaced bullshit—Red Linny probably wouldn't have killed him.

Killing Persons wasn't even in Linny's big plans when he got out of prison in '69, and began building a crime empire he'd started seven years earlier in Attica. The juvenile court judge had given that two-faced John Shaft the choice of being tried as an adult, or joining the military. The same fucking judge never gave Linny that choice. Between that damn judge and Shaft, who fucked everything up on the job they'd pulled together, Red Linny's life went into the toilet a month after his seventeenth birthday.

His frail build and his boyish face threatened to make Red Linny an easy target in Attica—fresh meat that would spend every day of his life sucking cock and taking it in the ass. He knew he'd be lucky if he made it two days inside the joint before he got all his teeth knocked out. Those big bad marys that staked their claim on new arrivals like him loved to knock out the teeth of their newly minted bitches. That way you couldn't bite down on the unwanted cocks being shoved in your mouth.

Red Linny knew this would be his fate. He'd barely survived juvenile detention, and that was only because of Cookie Venable and John Shaft. But neither of those unreliable motherfuckers would be in Attica to watch out for him. Other members of the Dam Aces were locked up, but Linny couldn't count on them anymore than he could count on Shaft or Cookie.

So it came to pass, that on his first day in Attica, before he could get turned out and passed around, Red Linny decided to become the baddest motherfucker behind bars. Walking through the yard on his way to being processed he felt all eyes on him. What none of them knew was that he was studying them, looking for just the right person to make the statement he needed to make.

Within six hours of being in Attica, Red Linny had

taken out his first victim. He picked the baddest, meanest looking nigger he could find, and he attacked. Up until that moment, he'd never thought about what it would feel like to kill someone else. He was surprised at how good it felt. It was an exhilarating rush—a surge of unbridled power that could only come from depriving another person of their life, fueled by the fear of those that had seen it all go down. They looked at him like he was crazy—like he was dangerous. And that's exactly what he wanted.

All of his life, Linwood Morton had been picked on and beaten up, or protected by someone else. But that night, after dinner, with a spoon he'd smuggled out of the cafeteria, Morton went from being the prey to the predator. He transformed from the weird-looking brainy kid in the Dam Aces—the one with lofty dreams of greatness—to the coldblooded killer that would never cower in fear again. By the next morning, no one in Attica dared to fuck with him. Seven years later, he was released back onto the streets with the power and connections to become a force to be reckoned with.

He hadn't planned to kill Bamma Brooks unless it was absolutely necessary. Brooks just happened to be in the wrong place at the wrong time, and Red Linny wasn't even sure if the man had gotten a good look at him. It would've been easy enough to have someone kill Brooks while he lay in a coma. Shit, he could've paid an orderly to do that. But that wasn't the plan.

The plan had been to wait and see if anyone came calling on Brooks—anyone who might still be loyal to Persons. This would've made things that much easier for Morton, as he knew cats like Nicky Barnes and Fleetwood King would never come paying a visit. Those motherfuckers had their place in the changing landscape, which didn't mean shit to Morton—they were just pawns in the game. It was the holdouts that he worried about—those old Negroes that still held a sense of loyalty to the way things used to be. Those old niggers that started running moonshine down south, before migrating up north to run numbers, pussy, and dope, were dinosaurs that hadn't figured out their time had passed. He'd hoped the remaining holdouts might reveal themselves.

Instead, the stupid asshole Koblanski fucked everything up by taking things into his own hands. That dumb motherfucker couldn't even get a simple hit right. How the fuck do you fuck up killing some-one that up until a few hours earlier had been in a coma?

Fortunately, like all great leaders, Red Linny had planned ahead. He had close to a dozen soldiers sta-tioned, round-the-clock, at key places throughout Harlem. One of those spots was close to the home of

Moses Moseley, who didn't pose much of a threat, but remained one of the few unknown factors in Harlem.

When the call came that Brooks had been spotted in a police car headed toward Moseley's home, Red Linny dispatched three men to take care of things. Three should've been enough to go up against an old man, his grandsons, and the fresh-out-of-a-coma Brooks.

Three hadn't been enough to deal with John Shaft. Morton hadn't figured on Shaft being there, fucking everything up like he always did. Now, they were all in the wind—Brooks, Shaft, and the Moseleys, who wouldn't take kindly to being attacked. The Moseleys were out of the game, but they still had power, especially down South, where Bluehand Geechie's name and legacy still carried weight.

Things had been going so well—the plan coming together. Big bad Knocks Persons was dead and buried, and less than a week later, the power struggle had begun. Through his connections, Morton had three shipments of heroin arriving—all going to different dealers. This would cause shit to heat up. A turf war was imminent. And then the guns would arrive, and Morton could start supplying the armies looking to control the smack trade. He would get rich supplying everyone with the dope they were fighting over, and the guns being used in the fight. The only problem was that Koblanski was an idiot, and Shaft had turned up unexpectedly.

Red Linny had planned to set things up so Shaft would kill Koblanski and the other cops, but that wasn't going to happen—there wasn't enough time for that plan to come together. He felt a wave of disappointment knowing that his carefully crafted plan would never see the light of day. He loved making detailed plans—he really did. At the same time, there was something special about letting the animal out of the cage with no real plan, just a hunger for blood. That's how he handled things that first day back in Attica. He didn't have much of a plan—just an idea. He knew what he had to do, but not how to do it. Then he let himself go, giving into what was in his heart. And that's how he'd handle it with Shaft.

# THIRTY-TWO

Shaft sat on the floor of the maintenance closet, trying to make sense of his world. The closet, which was really more of a small room, was located in the rear corridor of the building that housed Shaft's office. The door didn't lock from the inside, but with his back pressed against the door, Shaft had barricaded himself inside, with a single bulb hanging from the ceiling, and the box of truth Knocks Persons's had left behind.

It had taken Shaft hours to get from Harlem back to midtown—a paranoid journey of backtracking, watching his every step, and constantly looking over his shoulder. He didn't bother going to his office, knowing full well that the entrance to his building was being watched. Likewise, there was a good chance someone was waiting for him in his tiny third floor office. Fortunately, he didn't need anything in the office itself. All he needed was the box he'd hidden in the closet.

Shaft stood across the street from the adult book-store that served as his secret entrance to the rear hall-way of his office building, watching for more than thirty minutes. He had to be sure that no one was eye-balling the porn store. And even after thirty minutes, he wasn't completely sure.

He kept his head low—like most of the guys that entered the bookstore—moving quickly to the back. He pause for a few seconds, making sure he wasn't being followed, then quickly slipped into the back hallway.

Secure and relatively safe inside the tiny storage room, Shaft opened the box Knocks Persons left for him. That's when he started to feel the world collapsing all around him. The more he dug through the box, the more Shaft's world collapsed.

Under a different set of circumstances, the con-tents of the box would've seemed like a collection of random bullshit. Aside from the letter Persons had left Shaft, and the bundle of cash, everything else seemed to have no value—at least no value before his world had started to change. Before Moses Moseley said that he knew Shaft's father.

The contents of the box primarily consisted of two things—photographs and composition notebooks. The photos were all from the personal life of Knocks Persons, starting sometime in the mid-1940s, after he'd returned from the war. Names and dates were written on the back of each photo, but Shaft didn't bother to study the pictures too carefully, instead concentrating on the notebooks.

The notebooks were the kind used by students and made by Mead—one hundred sheets, wide ruled. There were more than a dozen notebooks in the box, each one filled with the clean, elegant handwriting of Knocks Persons—page after page of his personal journals.

It would not have been that long ago that Shaft would've been surprised to find out Knocks Persons had kept a journal. Likewise, he would've been surprised by the rough man's penmanship, or the almost poetic way his thoughts flowed out on the pages of each notebook. But that was before the world started to collapse, and John Shaft began to fully realize how much he didn't know.

At first, Shaft didn't know what he was looking for in the journals. He knew Knocks left the personal writings to him for a reason, but that reason wasn't clear at first. Shaft skimmed the journals, being drawn deeper and deeper into the like of Persons. There were names he recognized, like Bumpy Johnson, Bluehand Geechie, and other Harlem gangsters whose names were familiar.

Only half paying attention to what he read, Shaft

realized he was being let in on the inner workings of the Harlem underworld. At another time, under other circumstances, he would've been more fascinated by what he read. But in the moment, sitting in cramped closet, hiding from unknown killers, Shaft had little interest in history. All of that changed when he came across a single name—Koblanski.

The name jumped out at him from off the page. Shaft flipped back to the beginning of the journal entry, dated September 16, 1946. Persons started the entry writing about the growing tension between himself and Bumpy Johnson. Shaft had picked up bits and pieces of the conflict between the two men from earlier entries that he'd read. From that standpoint, there was nothing new to be gleaned from the entry, until he got to the passage that read:

> "The problem with Johnson is nothing new, and does not concern me at this time. I am, however, concerned with a dirty cop that has been making his presence known. Bluehand Geechie warned me personally of an officer named Koblanski who had been putting the squeeze on his operation. Koblanski seems to have a tax on every crew north of 110th Street. If this

were a case of a lone greedy cop,
or even a small group of them, I
would not give it another thought.
But the truth of the matter is that
Koblanski is part of a much larger
organization in the department."

Shaft continued to read, looking for more entries related to Koblanski, which began to appear with growing frequency. Backed by his fellow officers and a few detectives in the Harlem precinct, Koblanski was shaking down nearly every operator uptown. In addition to taking their cut, Koblanski and his crew were knocking over operators outright. To read Persons's entries, Koblanski and his crew of cops were more of a problem than Italians ever were. "If the Italians step too far out of line, we can always go to war with them," Persons wrote. "There's no going to war with the police. They kill one of our runners, and what can we do to retaliate? Nothing."

The more he read, the more Shaft came across mentions of Koblanski. *Is this why Knocks left me all of this stuff?* Shaft wondered. *Did he think it was Koblanski that was going to kill him?*

Bamma Brooks told Shaft that Red Linny Morton had killed Persons—which Shaft had yet to completely believe or process. Maybe Brooks had been wrong.

After all, it seemed clear to Shaft that Persons believed his death would be at the hands of Koblanski. Why else would Persons leave the journals to Shaft?

That's what made most sense to Shaft, until he stumbled across a passage that made his blood run cold.

> "My good friend Quick Johnny is dead. Koblanski killed him."

# THIRTY-THREE

Shaft felt like a fool for not having noticed the name written in the journals of Knocks Persons sooner. Flipping through the pages he had skimmed earlier, there was the name, staring at him time and time again. Quick Johnny. His father.

What he had barely paid attention to before, suddenly became the most important thing in the world. More important than whoever killed Knocks Persons. More important than anyone out gunning for Shaft. Cramped in a maintenance closet, reading the pages of Knocks Persons's journal, John Shaft read about his father—a man he had never known.

As he carefully read all the journal entries he'd skipped over earlier, Shaft lost track of time. Every word of every entry took on newfound importance, because each word gave him greater insight into Persons. This insight gave each mention of his father a deeper meaning. For Shaft, it felt like the more he knew Persons, the better he could interpret the gangster's impression of Quick Johnny.

Knocks Persons and Quick Johnny met in 1945, just after Persons returned from the war—the same year Shaft was born. Knocks was twenty-five, working as hired muscle for Moses Moseley, when he met Johnny, a nineteen-year-old running numbers for Moseley's older brothers. Throughout the journals there were brief mentions of Johnny, many of them detailing his clashes with Koblanski and other corrupt cops. These passages began to paint the picture of a young man unafraid to stand up for himself—of someone Knocks Persons admired.

Shaft read everything up to the journal entry about his father's death. He stopped, incapable of reading more, emotionally spent. He knew the journals contained more information, but his brain couldn't process anymore. Shaft let the composition notebook slip from his hands and fall to the floor.

Without giving it any thought, Shaft reached into the box and pulled out the stack of photographs that, much like the journals, he'd only paid minimal attention. Absentmindedly, he flipped through the pictures, when he came across a picture of himself. Only it wasn't him. For the first time in his life, John Shaft saw his father.

The resemblance between Shaft and the man in

the photo was uncanny. If he'd had any doubt that Quick Johnny was his father, the picture put an end to any and all debate. There were more pictures, each one of them showing a man that looked so much like Shaft he almost got confused. One picture stood out more than any other. It was the picture of Quick Johnny, smiling broadly, holding an infant in his arms. Standing next to Quick Johnny was a young woman who looked equally happy. Shaft only had a few memories of the woman, and none of them included her looking so happy. Try as he might, Shaft had no memories of his mother, Hazel Shaft, ever smiling.

Shaft didn't notice when he started to cry. With the contents of Knocks Persons's box of truth strewn over the floor of the maintenance closet, John Shaft found himself lost in a world of emotion he had never been in before. It was a land far beyond the jungles and ghetto streets haunted by the ghosts of all those he'd killed. It was a place of raw emotional truth, where nothing could dim the light or drown out the sound that overloaded your senses. It was the place where grown men found the little boys they used to be— where the seeds of personal destruction are planted, and left to take bloom at a later date.

He hated Knocks Persons for leading him to this place. This was worse than standing over the bullet-riddled corpses of nameless Viet Cong. This was worse than lying in bed with a woman whose name you couldn't remember. This was worse than walking through Times Square and reminding yourself you weren't that crazy because you weren't taking a shit on the sidewalk. This was worse than getting shot by some teen thug, or being on the run from crooked cops. This was worse than losing the love of your life. This was worse than anything.

At some point, Shaft cried himself to sleep in the cramped maintenance closet. He dreamed of killing and fucking. He dreamed of the life he might have had if Quick Johnny hadn't died so young. A life were Hazel Shaft hadn't fallen down the stairs and broken her neck. A life where Johnny and Hazel lived happily ever after, and their son grew up to be normal.

He woke up, stiff and sore, gathered up the contents of the box, and placed it back in its hiding place. Maybe, if Shaft was lucky, he'd forget it existed.

# THIRTY-FOUR

Shaft's mind was in a cloudy haze. Try as he might, he couldn't find his focus, which led to doubt and uncertainty, both of which would get him killed in the very near future if he wasn't careful. Even if he wanted to, he couldn't hide out in the maintenance closet forever. The box he had hidden in the ventilation shaft called out to him a bit too loudly from this distance, and he needed to get away. The problem was that he didn't really know where to go, or what to do. He tried to sort out the events of the last week or so—everything that happened after he answered that late night call from Knocks Persons. His entire world started to fall apart the moment he answered the goddamn phone.

Of course, that wasn't entirely true. His world had been falling apart for a long time—the signs had always been there—he just managed to ignore them all. Between the Johnnie Walker and the endless stream of chicks with their legs open, calling out his name while he couldn't remember theirs, Shaft had plenty of ways to ignore the fucked up truth of his life. Now he had more bullshit to deal with, and not a bottle of whiskey or an open pair of legs anywhere to distract him.

After what seemed like a ridiculously long time, Shaft decided to leave the cramped quarters of the maintenance closet. He snuck out of the building the same way he snuck in—exiting through the entrance of the adult bookstore on 45th Street. He carefully made his way up Seventh Avenue and around to 46th, where he stood across the street from his office building, keeping an eye open for anyone that looked like a cop.

A car parked in front of the building may or may not have been an unmarked police vehicle. Shaft couldn't be sure, though he was pretty damn sure, and that was good enough for him to be extra cautious. At first, the unmarked car seemed too obvious, but that didn't stop Shaft from playing it safe. If there were cops looking for him, the two places they'd stake out were his office and his apartment.

Shaft stood at the phone booth on the corner of Seventh Avenue and 46th Street, looking across the street and down the block at the entrance to his office building. The car parked in front taunted him. He needed to know for sure if there were cops looking for him, or if the only thing he had to worry about were the killers of Knocks Persons. He also needed to get in touch with Vic Anderozzi. *Maybe Vic has had better luck than me*, he thought to himself.

Shaft dropped a dime into the pay phone and dialed the number of the No Name, the bar on Jane Street, across from his apartment. If cops were staking out his apartment, you'd be able to see them from the No Name. If those cops needed to take a piss break, the No Name was the nearest bathroom they could use. And if there were cops, Rollie Nickerson, the bartender at the No Name Bar, would notice them.

An aspiring actor who sold weed on the side, Rollie was the most paranoid person Shaft knew. Rollie spent most of his time at the bar, either working, selling weed, or just hanging out. Any suspected undercover police activity near the No Name, and Rollie would assume it was aimed at him. Rollie also liked to think of himself as Shaft's sidekick—the Dr. Watson to Shaft's Sherlock Holmes. He had this view of himself, even though he'd never worked a case with Shaft, nor had any interest in working a case. The most Rollie ever did—aside from introducing Shaft to horny chicks at the bar—was to take the occasional message, usually from one of the chicks after Shaft screwed them.

When he'd been dropped off near Harlem Hospital, Shaft told Anderozzi to leave any messages with Rollie at the No Name. It wasn't the first time Shaft and Anderozzi had used Rollie to convey messages back and forth. Other lines of communication could be compromised—phone lines bugged—but because no one else knew about the Rollie Nickerson connection, it made sense to use him from time to time.

"John, hey man, I'm glad you called," Rollie said. "That friend of yours—the cop—he left a message. Wants you to call him."

"Great. Thanks," said Shaft, writing down the number Rollie gave him on the back of a matchbook cover. "You notice anyone hanging out the last day or two?"

"You mean like the cops that've been staking out your place?" asked Rollie.

"That's exactly what I mean."

"Yeah, these guys aren't even trying to be undercover about it. That's how I know they aren't lookin' to bust me," Rollie said with a laugh.

Shaft asked a few specifics about the cops staking out his place—like if they had been asking around about him, maybe flashing his picture. Rollie had nothing more to share, but he'd shared enough. He'd confirmed Shaft's suspicions—there were cops staking out his apartment. And that meant that the car in front of his office building belonged to cops as well.

He started to call the number Anderozzi had left for him, when an idea popped in his head. It dawned on Shaft that the cops looking for him didn't know him very well. They were acting as if they thought he was too stupid to consider that they might be staking out his pad or his office. This meant that they were lazy and obvious in their approach, which might be things he could use to his advantage.

He dropped another dime into the slot of the pay phone, and instead of dialing the number Anderozzi had given Rollie, he dialed another number. Shaft had a hunch he wanted to play. If he was right, it could give him an advantage over the cops looking for him. If he was wrong, at the very least he might get to hear a friendly voice.

"We Don't Sleep So You Can," answered the familiar voice of Mildred.

Shaft breathed a sigh of relief. Mildred answering the phone meant that some tiny shred of his life still made sense. "Mildred, this is John Shaft."

"Oh," said Mildred, pausing for a brief moment. "Hello, sir."

Mildred called him sir. She never called him sir. Something was wrong—maybe the cops had called looking for him, just as he suspected.

"Mildred, by any chance have the police been

looking for me?" asked Shaft.

Mildred paused for a brief second before answering, "Sorry, sir, you don't have any messages at this time."

He heard it in her voice—in the slow, measured way she answered his question. He heard it, and he knew.

"Are cops there right now, in the office?" Shaft asked.

"Yes, sir, I can double check to make sure I'm not missing any messages," Mildred said.

Shaft fought to contain his anger. It was one thing to have the police out looking for him—presumably to kill him. He could live with that. But the thought of corrupt cops, hovering around the cramped offices of the We Don't Sleep So You Can, harassing Mildred, that got his blood boiling. His mind kicked into high gear, quickly putting a plan into action.

"Mildred, I'm sorry they dragged you into this," said Shaft. "Don't let them know that I know they are there. But when they ask if I said anything, tell them that I said I'll be up in Harlem working on a case."

"Okay, sir," said Mildred, before hanging up the phone.

Shaft imagined the older woman—or at least the image he'd created in his mind—being bullied by the police. His anger started to rise. The police were waiting for him at his office, and at his apartment, and they weren't looking to question him. He was being hunted by rouge cops looking to do him in, but not before they found out where to find Detective Harry Townes.

Like a statue, he stood in the phone booth, patiently watching the front of his office building. He didn't check his watch, but his best estimate told him three minutes had passed. Three minutes would've been long enough for whatever communication system Koblanski and his men had in play to do its trick. Maybe they were communicating by way of a private channel over their police radios, or maybe they were using phones. Hell, they could've been using carrier pigeons, although that didn't seem to be the most time efficient.

A few minutes passed, and two men walked out of the building—one that had no doubt been waiting in his office, the other had likely been waiting in the lobby on the first floor. Shaft took them to be cops, and the fact that they got into the car parked out front—the same car Shaft suspected of being an unmarked police vehicle—only confirmed all of his suspicions.

Someone had been standing over Mildred's shoulder. She had told them that Shaft was up in Harlem somewhere, working a case, and they sent the word out. The assholes that had been staking out his offices had gotten a call of some sort—"He's somewhere in Harlem." Somewhere down in the Village, another group of assholes had gotten the same call. This meant that whoever was looking for him would now be concentrating their efforts across 110th Street. They would be asking questions in all the bars, and on all the street corners, and cruising past suspected spots, looking for him; thinking the entire time that they were ahead of him, because they knew John Shaft was in Harlem working on a case.

An angry, cynical smile crept across Shaft's face. The cops thought they were the hunters and Shaft was the prey. He took great comfort in knowing how wrong they actually were. He'd set the trap, and they were heading into it. For the first time in what felt like a very long time, he felt in control.

He reached into his pocket and pulled out another dime. He dialed the number Anderozzi had left for him. As the phone started to ring, Shaft was already planning his next move.

# THIRTY-FIVE

"We're in over our heads," said Detective Harry Townes. "You know that, right?"

Vic Anderozzi nodded his head without saying a word. He was, in fact, over his head, drowning in an ocean of bullshit. He sat in an uncomfortable chair, in a cheap motel room a few blocks from Yankee Stadium. The sound of a hooker screwing a john in the next room made it difficult to concentrate, and the lingering smell of cigarettes made him want to vomit.

Townes lay on an old mattress that had undoubtedly absorbed its fair share of cum. A few feet away, the detective that Anderozzi and Townes had dragged from the wrecked cop car, sat on the floor, his mouth gagged, his hands cuffed to a radiator that no longer worked.

Townes knew the other detective from the Harlem Precinct. Tom Sullivan was part of a precinct full of corrupt cops, all of whom answered to Koblanski. All of the Sullivans and Koblanskis on the force made it especially difficult for honest, hard-working cops like Townes and Anderozzi to make a difference. Now, the corrupt cops were making it hard for them stay alive.

Several hours had passed since Anderozzi had checked into the Homerun Motel. He'd left Townes to sleep on the bed, and Sullivan chained to the radiator, while he went outside to gather his thoughts. He found a diner down the street from the motel, ordered some food to go, and made a few phone calls while the order was being prepared. The first call was to his wife. The second, significantly longer call was to Archie Edmonds, a detective in the department's Internal Affairs Division.

"What do you know about a Stan Koblanski, works out of the Harlem Precinct?" asked Anderozzi.

"Koblanski is like an inoperable tumor," said Edmonds, as he went on to describe Koblanski's long list of alleged offenses.

"Some of his guys tried to take out another cop, guy by the name of Harry Townes."

"No shit? I know Townes. He's good police. He okay?" asked Edmonds.

"Okay enough," said Anderozzi. "We got our hands on one of Koblanski's stooges, and we need to pass him off to someone."

Anderozzi gave Edmonds the address of the

Homerun Motel. He wasn't sure if bringing Internal Affairs was a good idea or not—even someone he trusted as much as Edmonds, but Anderozzi had no other options.

The third call Anderozzi made was in an attempt to get word to Shaft. He returned to the motel room with food and coffee, where he waited for Townes to wake up, Sullivan to regain consciousness, and Edmonds to arrive.

With Townes awake, Anderozzi no longer had to sit in silence, listening to the traffic that drove past or the hookers in the surrounding rooms. Townes's assessment that they were in over their heads made Anderozzi long for the quiet of the dingy room, and the surrounding chorus of fat slobs grunting as they pumped away on prostitutes faking orgasms.

"Yeah, we're in over our heads, but it's not finished yet. We can get out of this," said Anderozzi, forcing himself to sound optimistic. The call he made to Internal Affairs would either prove to be the cavalry they needed, or their ultimate undoing. Anderozzi had hoped for the former.

The phone next to the bed rang. Townes jumped with a start.

Anderozzi got up from his chair and answered the phone. "Yeah."

"Got your message," said Shaft on the other end of

the line.

Anderozzi filled Shaft in on what had happened since they parted company. Shaft gave Anderozzi an abbreviated version of what happened to him as well.

"Sounds like we've both had our fair share of excitement," Anderozzi said.

"Sounds like it."

"I don't know about you, Johnny, but I'm ready for this party to be over."

"You can say that again," said Shaft. "Not sure what you've got planned, but I'm getting ready to head back up to Harlem. There's a killer up there waiting to be caught."

# THIRTY-SIX

Word had come down that John Shaft was some-where in Harlem, and Stan Koblanski breathed a sigh of relief. In all of his years on the force, he couldn't think of a spade that he'd never even met—or even seen in person—who'd given him more trouble than Shaft. Although, if he were to be completely honest with himself, Koblanski knew that Shaft was only part of a much bigger problem. That bigger problem came in the form of Red Linny Morton, who had set every-thing in motion.

If it hadn't been for Morton taking out Knocks Persons, there wouldn't have been a problem with Shaft—or Townes for that matter. Townes had proven to be a bigger problem than Shaft, and now he was in the wind, thanks to Anderozzi. Much like Shaft, Townes and Anderozzi were only symptoms of a dis-ease. The disease itself was Morton, a cold-blooded psychopath that had served his purposes, but had outlived his usefulness.

Koblanski had made a lot of money off Morton, but this latest caper had come with a risk that far exceeded the reward. It didn't matter what kind of connections Red Linny had, Koblanski decided it was time to put the rabid dog down.

He made several calls to his most trusted men, rallying his troops up to Harlem, where they would find Shaft, and in turn find Townes. Shaft and Townes were dead men. And if the unreasonable Vic Anderozzi couldn't be reasoned with, he'd join them. Koblanski had no compunctions about taking out that sanctimonious guinea, and he wrestled with killing him just for the fuck of it. He'd for sure make it happen if he could get the three of them together, along with Red Linny. Then he'd be eliminating his biggest headaches in one move. After it was all done, he'd put in his retirement papers.

Koblanski sent word to Red Linny that Shaft was somewhere in Harlem. He also let it be known that they needed to talk about the upcoming deals going down. Koblanski had been providing protection to Red Linny for long enough, without knowing the criminal's connections. In the past, it didn't matter, so long as Morton made the proper pay offs. But as Koblanski thought more about getting rid of Red Linny, the more he realized there was an opportunity staring him in the face.

Cocaine and heroin had little interest for him. There was enough of it moving through Harlem that he could shake down any dealer or supplier, and make money. If didn't matter that Red Linny was waiting on a shipment that would position him to be the biggest supplier in Harlem—Koblanski wanted nothing to do with that business. No, the business Koblanski wanted a real piece of—the thing that would keep him flush in cash long after he retired—was the sale of guns.

He didn't know all the details of Red Linny's plan, but Koblanski knew there was a major shipment of guns coming in from Miami, either by way of Cuba, or perhaps Haiti. Morton had never shared his plans with Koblanski, but it didn't take a rocket scientist to figure it all out. Red Linny would provide dope to all the key dealers in Harlem. Without Knocks Persons calling the shots, turf wars would erupt as different players vied for power. Then those same dealers that were at war would turn to Red Linny, their dope supplier, to sell them guns. All Koblanski needed was to know who was supplying the guns, and he could easily take over the business. It would be that simple. And with his guys on the force, he could peddle guns anywhere in the city, and the money would roll in. Next to real estate, he couldn't think of a more sound investment.

It had been a trying week, there was no getting around that. But things were starting to finally turn around. It would only be a matter of time before everything making Koblanski's life difficult was just a distant memory. He could sit back and enjoy the good life. That would have to wait, however, until he finished cleaning up this little mess, which would require making more of a mess—it meant people had to die. The thought of killing anyone didn't bother Koblanski, as long as it was in service to him living a better life.

# THIRTY-SEVEN

For someone that hated Harlem as much as he did, Shaft spent far too much time there. Being the only black private dick operating in the city meant that he had a lock on white clients too scared to venture into the jungle. He paid the rent on both his apartment and his office just by investigating insurance claims in Harlem, even though he couldn't stand venturing up-town. When he died, and went to Hell—as he figured he would—Shaft knew that his damnation would be to walk the streets of Harlem for all eternity.

He crossed Adam Clayton Powell Jr. Boulevard and made his way to Small's Paradise. Anyone looking for anyone would make a stop at Small's, it was one of those spots in Harlem that served as an axis upon which many lives revolved. Small's Paradise was just one of several places Shaft made an appearance, as he carefully made his way through Harlem, taking great care to be seen at places where he would be recognized. To anyone that didn't know better, it appeared that he was simply making the rounds, stopping at various cocktail lounges and restaurants. He talked to bartenders and barflies, all of whom knew him, as did the street vendors and the hustlers. In the hierarchy of fame on the streets, Shaft ranked just below famous athletes, but above politicians, holding his own with the biggest of gangsters and the meanest of motherfuckers. Spiro Agnew or John Lindsay could walk through Harlem, and no one would recognize them as anything other than some dumb crackers somewhere they didn't belong. The same wasn't true for John Shaft.

Every place he stopped, every person he talked to, Shaft took great care to survey his surroundings. He kept his eyes open for anyone that looked like a cop, which wasn't too hard to do in this part of town. Sooner or later word would make it through the grapevine that he was in one place or another, and it helped that the cops were already looking for him. No doubt, someone Shaft had stopped to talk to would've already been questioned by one of the corrupt pigs looking for him. Shaft was leaving a trail of breadcrumbs anyone could follow.

Shaft's biggest concern, however, wasn't the police. He wanted them to find him. No, his biggest concern was the other players in this deadly game. It was who-

ever had killed Knocks Persons, and whoever attacked
the home of Moseley. Whoever had done that was
more of a threat than the police, because Shaft didn't
know them—at least not for sure. Other than what
Bamma Brooks had told him, Shaft had nothing to go
on—he didn't know who he was looking for. Then he
saw one of them.

At first he thought it was just another tough kid
from the mean streets of Harlem. They were everywhere—Shaft had even been one of them a long time
ago. Under normal circumstances, he might not have
even noticed the kid, or simply dismissed him, but
that was before everything that had gone down at
Knocks Persons's home. Before he'd come face to face
with a teenage gunman. Now, in light of all that happened, Shaft had become more aware, which is how
he spotted the kid.

The kid couldn't have been more than fifteen, and
otherwise nondescript, except for the hardened look
in his eyes. Shaft recognized those eyes, because he
had them himself growing up. They were the eyes of a
man who had already seen too much, while he was still
just a boy.

Shaft saw the kid for the first time on 125th Street,
and thought nothing of him. He'd spotted the kid a
second time on his way to Small's Paradise near 135th,
and it struck Shaft as odd that he would see the same

kid in such a short time span. It wasn't until Shaft stepped out of Small's Paradise, and saw the kid for a third time that he realized he was being followed.

Without acknowledging that he'd spotted his tail, Shaft continued further north in to Harlem. The kid followed from nearly a block back, and all Shaft would have to do to lose him would be to make a break for it, cut down an intersecting street, and dash into any one of a number of apartment buildings. That would work, unless, of course, there was another tail.

Across the street, Shaft spotted another young man—this one a bit older. He matched Shaft's pace, so much so that the private detective almost laughed. These kids might've thought they were doing a good job of tailing him, only they weren't—not by a long shot. They were awkward and obvious, a bit too eager, with no sign of patience. Shaft suddenly thought of himself at that age, fumbling around with Wonder Wanda, uncertain of how to do what he so desperately wanted to do. Wonder Wanda had taken the lead, not in a way that diminished his burgeoning masculinity, but one that encouraged it.

In that moment, Shaft missed Wonder Wanda more than he ever missed her before. Not in the way someone missed an old lover, but in the way someone missed an entire part of their life. He missed her the way people missed their youth, even when their youth had been a nightmare of violence and poverty. Because despite all the things he experienced in his youth, and all that he thought he knew back then, he'd come to realize that things could get worse. Growing up in all those foster homes, all the fights while he was in the Dam Aces, these experiences and so many more had toughened him up and laid the foundation for who he'd become, but none of them were as bad as what he would see and do as he grew older. Even with his time spent in juvenile detention, even with the fights in the alleys of Harlem, even with mugging tourists in Central Park, none of it compared to the dead Viet Cong at his feet.

When he was younger, Shaft thought he understood violence the same way a virgin thinks they understand sex. It wasn't until he got to Vietnam that he realized how unrealistic his perceptions were when it came to the pain and suffering one person could inflict on another. He felt a wave of nausea at the thought of teaching the young men following him a real lesson about what it meant to be violent. Not only could he kill either of them with his bare hands, he might well have to—and that made him angry.

Shaft bolted across the street, moving toward the older of the two kids. It took the boy a second to realize what he was doing, but by then it was too late. Shaft saw the kid reach behind his back for something, and as he grabbed the young man by the collar, he knew what the next move had to be. Holding firmly to the young man's collar with one hand, Shaft spun the kid around and snatched the gun from the waist of his pants. Shaft then whipped his prisoner around one-hundred-eighty degrees, using him as a human shield, as the second kid came running from down the block.

"Hold it right there, kid," said Shaft.

The younger of the two kids stopped in his tracks. He held a gun that was almost too big to fit in his hand.

"Don't think for a second I won't kill either of you motherfuckers," growled Shaft. "Now get over here and give me that piece."

Shaft's attention was on the kid moving slowly toward him, which is why he didn't notice the car until it was right next to him. The front and rear passenger windows were rolled down, and the sawed off barrels of the shotguns pointing at him rested comfortably on the window edges.

"Get in the car, Johnny, or I'll have them open you up right here," said the driver.

Shaft could tell by the tone in Red Linny Morton's voice that he wasn't fucking around.

# THIRTY-EIGHT

Shaft recognized the old brownstone on 160th Street, even though the building had fallen into a state of disrepair since he'd seen it last, more than a decade ago. It had been one of the many places he'd called home during his youth—one of the many places he'd hoped never to see again. There was so much Shaft hated about Harlem—so many places, people, and things—that it made it easier for him to just hate the entire package. This building, the former location of some state-run home for boys, was part of an ugly life that had done its best to break John Shaft.

The car pulled to a stop in front of the old home. All of the houses on the block were either burned down or boarded up—long ago abandoned to the blight of urban decay. Several long chords ran from the brownstone to the nearest street lamp outside, stealing power to give life to something that by all rights was dead. It made Shaft think of Frankenstein's monster.

Red Linny led the way into the crumbling building, while Shaft, surrounded by a group of heavily armed teenagers, followed close behind. In a lifetime that seemed like someone else's nightmare, Shaft had once been the same age as the boys that now watched him carefully, fingers on the triggers of their weapons. In that lifetime, Shaft had been friends with Red Linny—womb-to-tomb niggers that had sworn an oath of brotherhood.

Bamma Brooks had told him that the killer of Knocks Persons was Red Linny, but Shaft didn't want to believe it. There was no reason for Red Linny to kill Knocks. At least there was no reason for the Red Linny that Shaft knew years ago to kill Knocks. But that was a different person—a person Shaft hadn't seen in more than ten years. That Red Linny hadn't been a killer. Then again, neither had that Shaft.

The last time Shaft saw Red Linny they both were seventeen and facing charges as adults. Rather than go to prison, Shaft opted for the Marines, and ended up in a country he'd never even heard of before. Red Linny was 4F, and didn't have the choice Shaft had.

A flood of memories crashed down on Shaft has he entered the old home. Inside the building looked worse than the outside. Trash and clutter littered the floor, while wallpaper peeled and hung like dead leaves on a tree, just waiting for a strong enough wind to shake them loose. A terrible stench lingered in the air—a mix of piss and garbage and body odor, with a whiff of poverty and despair.

"Like what you done with the place," said Shaft. "It's got an *Oliver Twist* feel to it."

Red Linny looked over his shoulder and sneered at Shaft, which only made the private detective want to laugh. Even with what Shaft knew was the very real threat of his imminent death, the entire thing had a comical feel to it. With his kinky red hair, pale skin, and clubfoot limp, Red Linny looked like a second-rate villain from the *Batman* television show they re-ran on Channel 11. The gang of teens Red Linny had working for him reminded Shaft of the ridiculous goons employed by Cesar Romero and Frank Gorshin, only crossed with the sad street urchins working for Fagin. Unable to control himself, Shaft started to laugh.

Red Linny turned to look at Shaft. "The fuck is so funny?" he asked, leading the way into what had been the communal living room of the group home. This was the room the boys had gathered in, pretending they had normal lives as they watched the black and white television set, or played checkers. The room was sparsely decorated with not much more than an easy chair and an old sofa. Light crept in through a dirt-streaked picture window along the far wall that over-looked a back alley.

"Just thinking about all the good times we had here," said Shaft. "What was the name of the cat who ran this place? You know—the one that always kept the candy in his pockets for the younger boys to get."

"Chester."

"That's right—Chester the molester," said Shaft. "You ever reach in and get any of that candy?"

Red Linny sat down in the easy chair that looked like it had been found in a dump, his back to the large picture window. He faced Shaft, who stood with a semi-circle of armed teenagers behind him. "You ain't half as funny as you think you are," said Red Linny.

"Everybody tells me that," Shaft said.

"You should listen to them."

"Something tells me it's a little late for that."

Red Linny started to laugh. "First funny thing I've ever heard you say."

"You gonna do me like you done Cookie Venable?" asked Shaft.

"No, not like Cookie. Got plans for you," said Red Linny. He snapped his fingers, and a moment later, another teen soldier showed up, placing a chair next to Shaft.

Red Linny motioned for Shaft to sit in a way that was more of a command than a request.

Shaft sat down on the creaky chair that must've been in an elementary school classroom thirty years earlier. The chair forced him to sit lower to the ground, with his knees up higher than was comfortable. Shaft wondered it was some kind of ploy to throw him off his game, or if this was the only other chair in the place.

"Is this where we play catch-up?" asked Shaft.

"I know all about you, Mr. Big Time Private Dick," said Red Linny.

"And you're still running around with teenagers," said Shaft. "What's the matter—can't find no grown folks to play with? I thought Attica would've made a man out of you."

"Nigger, don't ever talk to me about Attica. That place made me more of a man than you'll ever be," Red Linny said. His voice was quiet and calm, but Shaft could hear the anger that held it all together. He recognized that he was talking to a killer.

Shaft held up his hands in a gesture meant to make him look apologetic. He smiled, but not a smile of friendship so much as the toothy grin of a predator about to strike.

"Why you show up at Knocks Persons's place," asked Red Linny.

"He called," said Shaft. "Needed my help. Said someone was looking to do him in."

Red Linny nodded his head, a slight smile creeping across his face. "He sound scared?"

"No."

Red Linny's eyes narrowed, his smile turned to a frown. "How you know he wasn't scared?" he asked.

"I don't know," said Shaft. "But he didn't sound scared. You tell me—did he look scared before you killed him?"

The two men stared at each other, sitting in silence. Shaft fought the urge to survey the room as best he could, looking for possible escape routes. Looking away from Red Linny would be read as a sign of defeat in what was clearly some kind of showdown. Besides, the problem with escaping was that it meant violence, which meant likely killing one or more of Red Linny's teen soldiers. The thought of it bothered Shaft, even though he suspected the kids guarding him wouldn't hesitate to end his life.

"You wanna know why I killed that old motherfucker?" asked Red Linny.

"Knowing that you killed him is enough for me."

"Oh, that's enough? Enough for what?"

Shaft shrugged his shoulders. "The fuck you want from me, man?" he asked. "You want me to be scared? 'Cause I'm not. You think this is the first time some half-ass motherfucker had a bunch of teenagers pointing guns at me? You ain't got shit on Ho Chi Minh, and that fucker didn't scare me either."

"You trying to fuck with me to see if I'll slip up?" asked Red Linny. "Because if that's the case, let me tell you, that shit ain't gonna work. Ain't no slippin' to be done on my part. You about to die, John Shaft, and I'm about to enjoy the show."

"Thought you said you weren't gonna do me like you did Cookie."

"I'm not gonna do you like I did Cookie," said Red Linny. "Putting Cookie down was like putting down a horse with a broken leg. I made it as quick and painless as possible, so that dumb motherfucker wouldn't suffer."

"Got it," Shaft said. "You want me to suffer."

"There ain't enough sufferin' you can do to make up for the shit you did to me," said Red Linny. "I could peel off all your skin, and roll you in salt, and it wouldn't be enough."

"If that's the case, you might as well just kill me now, because it sounds like nothing is going to get you off."

"I already told you, someone else is gonna kill you for me."

"Really? Really, motherfucker? You're gonna have one of these kids do some shit you're too much of a pussy to do?" Shaft demanded.

"No, it won't be one of these kids that kills you,"

said a voice from behind Shaft.

Shaft turned around to see a man he recognized from the hospital, an older white man that could only be Stan Koblanski. He stood in the entrance to the room with five other men.

"We'll be the ones taking caring of you, boy," said Koblanski.

# THIRTY-NINE

The fact that Vic Anderozzi's car still ran was a surprise to him. The entire rear end had been smashed in, the muffler had fallen off, and the alignment was completely out of whack. As the car crossed back into Harlem from the Bronx, he was convinced it would die at any moment. But the car had a tenacity that mirrored the dogged determination of Harry Townes, who sat in the passenger's seat.

Anderozzi and Townes argued in the dingy room of the Homerun Motel, but it was a fight that didn't last long. Anderozzi felt Townes was in no shape for what was about to happen next, while Townes countered that the fight was his in the first place. In the end, Townes won—not so much because he was right, but because Anderozzi really didn't want to go it alone. He didn't know for sure what he was up against, and figured it was better to go into battle with someone else—even if that someone else was wounded and exhausted.

So rather than a prolonged argument, they left their prisoner handcuffed to the radiator, waiting for Archie Edmonds of Internal Affairs to show up, and prepared to kiss their careers—and possibly their lives—goodbye, as they headed across the river.

During their brief phone conversation, Shaft laid out his plan of action with Anderozzi. The plan was simple enough: show up in Harlem and let himself be seen until someone came to get him. It would either be Koblanski, or whoever killed Knocks Persons, and whichever the case, the other would show up in due time.

"What if they kill you straight off?" Anderozzi asked.

"They won't kill me until they're convinced I can't deliver Townes to them, which means I just need to bullshit them until you show up," answered Shaft.

Anderozzi drove his beat up car to 125th Street near the Apollo Theatre—the designated spot where he'd start following Shaft. From there, he and Townes would keep their distance while maintaining a watchful eye. Townes was the first to spot the kid following Shaft. Neither he nor Anderozzi had spotted the car that pulled up to Shaft until it was right next to him.

Anderozzi and Townes sat parked at the end of the block on 160th Street, keeping an eye on both the old brownstone Shaft had entered, and the street itself.

Everything had unfolded pretty much the way Shaft thought it would, right up to Koblanski showing up.

Two cars turned onto 160th, pulling to a stop close to the brownstone. Koblanski and two other detectives got out of one of the car, while another three got out of the second car. Anderozzi and Townes watched as Koblanski and five other detectives entered the dilapidated building.

"I'll be damned," said Townes, "it's going down just like Shaft called it."

"No one ever said the man wasn't good at what he does," said Anderozzi. "I just hope we can get him out of there alive."

# FORTY

Shaft lay on the filth-covered floor of the brownstone; blood pouring from what he figured was a broken nose. The detectives had been working him over for a solid four or five minutes—"softening him up"—while Koblanski asked the same questions over and over again. "Where's Townes? How much does he know?"

After a few minutes, it became clear Shaft wasn't going to talk. The detectives packed a mean punch, but no meaner than anything else he'd ever felt. Besides, Shaft knew that once he talked, his usefulness was over—they'd put a bullet in his skull and call it a day if they thought there was nothing left to get out of him.

Koblanski stooped down and leaned in close. Shaft could smell the cop's rancid breath and cheap aftershave. "Don't make this any harder on yourself, boy," Koblanski said. "Tell me what I want to know, and it will be quick and painless. Or, we can work on you until you wish you were dead."

Koblanski straightened up, and moved across the room to Red Linny, who stared out the window while the cops had been beating on Shaft.

Lying on the floor, Shaft counted at least ten guns in the room. Ten guns in one room, and that was just what he knew of for sure—it didn't include whatever else might be roaming around the rundown brownstone. There was no doubt that Morton's crew was well armed, as evidenced by the attack on Moses Moseley's home. Those machine guns had to be somewhere, and Shaft figured they weren't too far away.

If he was lucky, Anderozzi and Townes were outside, waiting for the right moment to storm the place and rescue him. But that was just two guns, which wouldn't make much of a difference in the broad scheme of things. It would be like Paul Newman and Robert Redford at the end of *Butch Cassidy and the Sundance Kid*. Shaft knew that if anyone started firing, there would be no getting out of the room alive.

The possibility of dying in a hail of bullets didn't bother Shaft that much. Everyone died at some point, and he'd avoided the grasp of the grim reaper enough to feel that he was living on borrowed time anyway. That wasn't what bothered him.

The thing that ate at his soul was the fact that he'd

never get a chance to wrap his hands around Koblanski's throat and choke the life out of him. Shaft could go to his grave a happy man with a broken nose, if only he could take Koblanski with him. But that wasn't going to happen. Koblanski was on the other side of the room, and Shaft was on the floor, surrounded by the five detectives, pleased with themselves for the beating they'd dished out. Shaft wouldn't be able to avenge the father he never knew.

The attention of the room had shifted from the cops working Shaft over to the conversation between Koblanski and Red Linny. Koblanski's men kept dutiful eyes on their boss, never noticing what Shaft saw going on behind them at the entrance to the room. What had been four of Red Linny's teen enforcers had multiplied to ten, all of them armed. A trap was being set that only Shaft seemed to notice—a massacre was getting ready to occur.

Shaft looked around the room, knowing that if he had any hope of escaping, that it would have to happen soon. As near as he could tell, there were only two options. The first would be to get past Red Linny's soldier boys, which wasn't going to happen without a bazooka. The other option was to make it out the window, which was only slightly less impossible. If the opportunity presented itself, Shaft would make a break for the window.

Across the room, the hushed whispers of Koblanski and Red Linny grew louder. Koblanski called Morton a tarbaby. Red Linny called the cop a dumb pollock. In that moment, with tensions quickly escalating, everything began to make sense to Shaft. He understood the real reason Knocks Persons had left him that damn box, and all that money to find his killer.

Standing less than twenty feet away, arguing over whatever it was they were arguing about, Shaft saw the ugliest of truths he had ever seen. Not just one truth, or even two, but so many truths that Shaft couldn't begin to process all of them—like a monstrous hydra with multiple heads, each filled with razor-sharp fangs, dripping with poison. It was the truth of what men like Knocks Persons and Stan Koblanski did to make money in Harlem, and it was what those truths had done to boys like John Shaft, Cookie Venable, and Red Linny Morton. It was the truth of hustlers and gangsters making ends meet to feed their families in a world that gave them few options outside of vice and sin for profit.

Knocks Persons hired Shaft to find his killer, when the truth was that Knocks had sewn the seeds of his own death. He had helped build the world of crime and violence that led to Linwood Morton becoming Red Linny. Knocks Persons wasn't looking for justice from beyond the grave. He wasn't even looking for revenge. He wanted some kind of absolution.

And then there was Koblanski, a monster who fed on the monster that destroyed the lives of so many people. There was no way of measuring the damage Koblanski had wrought over the years—the number of lives he'd ruined through his greed, which fed on the crime and despair of Harlem. Shaft was the byproduct of both Knocks Persons and Stan Koblanski almost as much as he was the child of Hazel Shaft and Quick Johnny Smith.

Shaft saw it all so very clearly. He saw himself so clearly.

The argument between Koblanski and Red Linny grew in intensity. Koblanski pulled out his gun. Red Linny's boys pointed their weapons at Koblanski. The detectives pointed their weapons at the boys.

Shaft watched it all with a morbid fascination. He didn't know for sure what was going on, but it appeared that the relationship between Red Linny and Koblanski had reached a crucial juncture. King Kong and Godzilla had come to a point where Monster Isle wasn't big enough for the two of them anymore.

"You think you can come in here and talk to me like this?" demanded Red Linny. "This is my place."

"This might be your place, but Harlem is mine," said Koblanski.

"Not anymore it isn't," said Red Linny. His statement was punctuated by the click-clack sound of guns being cocked.

Koblanski and his men finally noticed what Shaft had seen moments earlier. Red Linny's teen enforcers, their guns locked and loaded, had Koblanski and his fellow cops outnumbered by more than two to one.

"Now, any of you motherfuckers that don't want to die right this moment, I suggest you put your guns down," said Red Linny. For dramatic effect, Red Linny took Koblanski's weapon away and pointed it at him.

Even in the dimly lit room, Shaft could see Koblanski's face flush with anger. Koblanski was staring down the barrel of a losing proposition, and the corrupt cop knew it. His companions knew it as well. They all lowered their guns, letting them drop gently to the floor.

Red Linny felt a rush of excitement at the power he now held in his hands. He hadn't thought it would be possible to take out Koblanski and Shaft on his own. He didn't think he'd be the one to get to squeeze the trigger, and it had been a dark cloud looming over his head. That dark cloud had been replaced by sunshine and rainbows. Red Linny could hardly contain himself. His cock grew hard. He raised the gun to Koblanski's head, and blew a hole in it the size of his fist.

One of the other detectives shouted, as time seemed to screech to a halt. Shock, confusion, and fear registered on the faces of Koblanski's men as his lifeless body collapsed to the floor.

"And that's that," said Red Linny. He stepped over Koblanski's body, joining his enforcers at the entryway to the room. He aimed Koblanski's gun at the other cops. "You motherfuckers, get over in the corner."

The detectives backed up into the far corner of the room.

Shaft saw it coming even before it started. He scurried to grab one of the guns that had been dropped by the detectives, just as Red Linny's enforcers opened fire on the police.

Several shots tore into the brownstone from outside. Red Linny's gunmen turned their attention from the massacre in the house to the gunfire coming from the street, which Shaft assumed had to be Anderozzi and Townes.

The distraction of the additional gunfire gave two of the detectives time to hit the floor and recover their weapons. One took up a position behind the easy chair, the other behind the old, lumpy sofa. From their positions, they opened fire.

Shaft crawled on his belly as bullets flew overhead in every direction. The crossfire made staying alive an unlikely proposition, but his odds were still better than they'd been just a few moments earlier. His best chance of survival was the fact that everyone in the room was trying to kill someone other than him.

Rather than joining in on the gun battle, Shaft took advantage of the only escape route open to him—the one he had scoped out minutes earlier. He shot out the glass of the picture window, picked himself up off the floor, and dove out the window. He crashed hard on the concrete of the alley outside, the force of impact knocking the wind out of him.

Tuning out the pain, Shaft got to his feet, gun in hand, and ran toward the end of the alley. He felt a familiar burn as a bullet caught him in the arm. He whipped around to see Red Linny leaning out of the window, pointing a gun at him.

Shaft fired off several rounds, but Red Linny pulled back, ducking back inside. Shaft couldn't tell if he'd hit his mark. He stumbled back a few feet to the entrance of the alley, and then turned to run, just as several shots ricocheted off the wall next to him. He dashed out of the alley, and rounded the corner back onto 160th Street.

Anderozzi and Townes were in defensive positions behind their damaged car. Neither of the police detectives was firing into the brownstone. Instead, they were hunkered down, waiting for the shooting to stop. Townes was the first to see Shaft at the end of the block. He motioned for Shaft to hold his position.

Shaft sat on the front steps of the building at the end of the block. There were no more shots being fired, only the sound of approaching police sirens. He wondered for a moment whose side the cops would be on. If they were part of Koblanski's crew of corrupt pigs, things were about to go from bad to worse. He wondered who was left alive inside the brownstone, if anyone might have gotten away. For all he knew, Red Linny could be running down the same alley, in the opposite direction, making good his escape. If that were the case, Shaft would be running into his old friend at some point in the future.

*I guess I'll find out soon enough*, Shaft thought to himself.

He looked down and examined the gunshot wound he took in the alley. Shaft began to laugh, knowing that for the time being there was nothing to worry about—everything was going to be fine. The bullet had hit him in his lucky spot.

# ACKNOWLEDGMENTS

This book would not be possible without Ernest Tidyman, who recognized the need for a black hero, and created John Shaft. Likewise, I owe a tremendous debt to Chris Clark-Tidyman, who trusted me when I said there were more Shaft stories to tell. Thanks to everyone at Curtis Brown Ltd, and to all the folks at Dynamite Entertainment, for letting me and Shaft do what needed to be done. Finally, a very special thanks to my cousin James Wilder-Hancock for introducing me to Jim A., who shared his experiences in the Vietnam War, allowing me an opportunity to better understand Shaft, and a generation of young men forged in combat.

# ABOUT THE AUTHOR

David F. Walker is a comic book writer, novelist, filmmaker, and creator of the pop culture magazine *BadAzz MoFo*. Walker's work includes the award-winning graphic novel *Shaft: A Complicated Man*, and the critically acclaimed Young Adult novel, *Super Justice Force*. He has written for Dynamite Entertainment, Dark Horse Comics, DC Comics, and Marvel Comics.

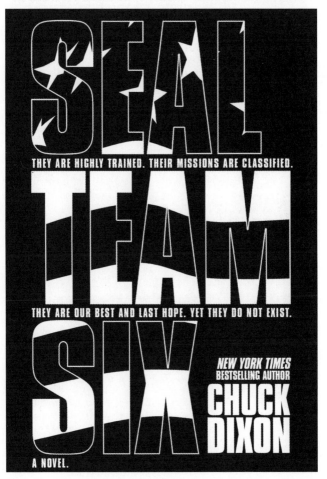